"*I remember a time when the taste of you was as sweet as passion fruit.*"

Whitney felt a whisper of fear move along her skin.

"But now you're a coldhearted woman, do you know that?"

"You'd better let go of me, Alex. I'm not going to put up with this kind of treatment from you."

His mouth twisted. "Spoken like a true lady of the manor." He leaned closer to her. "But you'll take whatever I dish out. And we both know it." A sly grin crossed his face. "What would you tell Daddy if his loan didn't come through?"

SANDRA MARTON says she has always believed in the magic of storytelling and the joy of living happily ever after with that special someone. She wrote her first romance story when she was nine and fell madly in love at the age of sixteen with the man she would eventually marry. Today, after raising two sons and an assortment of four-legged creatures, Sandra and her husband live in a house on a hilltop in a quiet corner of Connecticut.

Books by Sandra Marton

Don't miss any of our special offers. Write to us at the following address for information on our newest releases.

Harlequin Reader Service
P.O. Box 1397, Buffalo, NY 14240
Canadian address: P.O. Box 603,
Fort Erie, Ont. L2A 5X3

SANDRA MARTON

That Long-Ago Summer

Harlequin Books

TORONTO • NEW YORK • LONDON
AMSTERDAM • PARIS • SYDNEY • HAMBURG
STOCKHOLM • ATHENS • TOKYO • MILAN
MADRID • WARSAW • BUDAPEST • AUCKLAND

Harlequin Presents first edition January 1993
ISBN 0-373-11524-5

Original hardcover edition published in 1991
by Mills & Boon Limited

THAT LONG-AGO SUMMER

CHAPTER ONE

THE helicopter banked sharply as it came around the headland, but the updraught buffeted it anyway, just as Whitney had known it would. A giant hand seemed to lift the machine, then drop it gently before setting it on a level course again. The sensation was not unpleasant, it was more a reminder of nature's power than a threat, but it brought such a sudden flood of emotion that Whitney's throat tightened.

God, how she'd missed Hawaii. She'd known that, of course—it was nine years since she'd left home, but she'd never really stopped thinking about the jewellike beauty of the sea, the black sand beaches, and the soaring cliffs that thrust arrogantly from the ocean.

She'd expected to be happy to see it all again. What she hadn't counted on was the bittersweet remembrance that wrenched her heart.

There it was, just below her—Hina Beach, as beautiful as she remembered it. Sunlight shot the green Pacific with diamonds that sparkled in the white froth foaming against the black sand. Tall royal palms stood like sentinels before the cliff that rose so high it looked as if it might pierce the fat clouds that dotted the blue sky.

Whitney twisted in her seat and peered back at the beach as the 'copter rose above the *pali* and started inland. Hina had been her special place, her secret, and she wondered if it was possible that the last human footsteps to mar the black sand had been hers.

No, she thought suddenly, not just hers. The last time she'd come to Hina, she'd brought Andy with her. She'd led him through the ancient lava fields, along the lip of Kahuna Gorge, then down the steep bluff to the sea, and all the time he'd teased her, warned her that this secret spot of hers had better be as perfect as she'd promised.

Whitney had laughed with all the assurance of her sixteen years. "Of course it is," she'd said. "It's beautiful."

Andy had laughed, too, as he caught her in his arms. "Is it as beautiful as you? Because if it isn't, I'll make you pay."

She had tossed back her cloud of platinum hair and smiled up at him.

"And how will you do that?"

Andy's face had changed, darkening as he drew her close to his hard, tanned young body.

"I'll think of something," he'd whispered, and then his mouth had dropped to hers, his hands had slipped beneath her cotton T-shirt...

She started as a hand fell lightly on her shoulder. The helicopter pilot was asking her something, his brows raised in question, but it was lost in the whine of the blades above her head.

Whitney shook her head. "I can't hear you."

He nodded, leaned toward her, and spoke in her ear. "Are you okay?"

Whitney swallowed. No, she thought, no, I'm not. I'm sitting here conjuring up ghosts.

But she knew he was asking if she was feeling airsick, and she smiled and gave him a thumbs-up.

"I'm fine," she said.

He raised his thumb in return, then turned his attention back to the 'copter. Whitney sighed and leaned back in her seat.

Airsick, she thought with a faint smile. What would the pilot say if he knew she'd handled the controls of a single-engine Cessna, flying this same route, when she

was sixteen? She hadn't done any of the difficult stuff—
Kenny wouldn't let her land or take off—but he'd let
her take the stick more than once, not because she was
J.T.'s daughter but because she loved flying. He'd
promised to teach her, but somehow there'd never been
time. When she was seventeen, she'd gone to the
mainland, to boarding school. And she hadn't been back
to the Big Island since.

The 'copter dipped low over the rolling hills of the
Turner Ranch. Her stomach was beginning to knot:
they'd be landing in just a few minutes, and she wasn't
sure she was ready for whatever lay ahead. Her father
had to be ill—she'd tried and tried, but she couldn't come
up with any other explanation for his cryptic summons.

"Come home, Whitney," he'd written and the
scrawled plea had stunned her. Her father had never once
asked her that, not during all the years she'd been gone.
They had exchanged letters and phone calls, he visited
her each time he had business on the mainland, but
neither of them had ever mentioned the possibility of
her returning to the ranch. Now, suddenly, he'd made
this unlikely request, made it in a way that must have
humbled him almost as much as it had surprised her.

The pilot tapped her shoulder again, then pointed
ahead. Whitney nodded her understanding. There it was,
the landing pad, and the winding dirt road that led over
the gentle hills to the main house.

She swallowed nervously as the 'copter descended.
Dust swirled around them, and she caught a glimpse of
the Jeep bearing the Turner logo bouncing toward them
over the road. Her stomach knotted. But, when the
'copter had finally settled on the pad and the dust
cleared, she saw that it wasn't J.T. who'd come to meet
her, it was Kichiro.

By the time the old man pulled open the 'copter door
and grinned at her, Whitney was smiling.

"*Aloha*, missy," he said. "It is good to have you back."

"It's good to be back," she said, and, despite all her misgivings, she knew it was true.

Even after all these years, this was home.

Her father was sorry, but he'd been called away at the last minute, Kichiro said as they drove along the rutted dirt road that led to the main house. He'd said to tell her he'd be back as soon as he could, certainly long before dinner. Whitney reached over and touched the old man's arm.

"It's all right," she said. "I didn't really expect him to meet me."

Although that wasn't quite true. She hadn't expected a welcoming committee, but she was here, after all, at her father's specific request.

Considering the circumstances, he might have made it a point to...

"Kichiro? Is J.T. all right?"

The old man looked at her. "What do you mean, missy?"

Whitney put her hand on his. "If he's ill..."

He stared at her, his almond eyes unreadable. "No. He's not ill."

She felt a weight slide from her chest. "That's good. I don't know why I didn't think of it before, but..."

"Worried, maybe. But not sick."

Whitney frowned. "Worried? About what?"

"It's better that he tell you, missy."

"Tell me what? What's the big mystery?"

"No mystery." Kichiro stared straight ahead.

"Come on. It can't be..." Whitney leaned forward and shaded her eyes with her hand. "What is that, Kichiro?"

The old man didn't take his eyes from the road. "A fence," he said.

She grimaced. "Yes, I can see that. But why is it there?"

He puffed out his breath. "Houses," he said, as if the word were a toxin on his tongue.

She stared at him. "Houses? J.T.'s building houses on the ranch?"

Kichiro shifted uncomfortably. "Somebody else."

Whitney's eyes narrowed. "What are you talking about, Kichiro? Who else could build on Turner property?"

There was a long pause. "You ask, J.T.," he said finally, and from the way his jaw clamped Whitney knew she'd get nothing further.

Houses, she thought, craning her neck to peer back at the fence. Houses, on Turner land? Impossible.

The main house had not changed at all, she thought at first. It was cool and spacious, every window filled with specimens from her father's collection of rare orchids. But then she realized there were fewer servants. The woman who opened the front door was clearly doing double duty as cook as well as housekeeper: she had a dappling of flour on her broad bosom.

"Someone will bring your bags up later, miss. I'm afraid there's no one around just now."

Whitney shrugged. "It's just one suitcase," she said. "I'll take it up myself."

Stepping into her bedroom was like stepping into a time warp.

It was exactly as she'd left it, right down to the snapshots tucked into the dresser mirror and the tumble of stuffed animals on the canopied bed. She was surprised, at first. J.T. wasn't given to sentiment. She'd never given it any thought but, if she had, she'd have assumed he'd have had this room stripped of its childish mementoes long ago. But then she realized that he'd probably never even seen it after she'd left. The house was the province of the housekeeping staff. So long as it was kept clean and neat, her father had no interest in it.

Whitney walked slowly through the room, touching the back of the chair drawn up before the vanity, smiling at the faded corsage that lay on the mirrored glass, pausing finally before the triple mirror. So many memories, so many photographs, some of them fading after all these years.

There was one of the mother she didn't even remember, holding a tiny Whitney in her arms and smiling for the camera, her eyes already shadowed by the illness that would soon claim her.

And there was the picture of Nalani, the gentle *tutu* who had more than lived up to her Hawaiian name of "grandmother"—until J.T. had decided it was time his daughter had a proper European governess. She smiled as she reached for the next photo. How old had she been when that was taken? Five, perhaps, with her platinum hair drawn back in a proper knot, and only her dark blue eyes showing her pride in her first pony.

The photo fell from suddenly nerveless fingers as her glance slid to the last snapshot. Andy, she thought incredulously, it was Andy! But where had it come from? She'd burned every last picture of him, burned them and tossed the ashes to the sea.

Whitney's hand trembled as she reached out and took the snapshot from the mirror. Yes, it was Andy, captured by the camera's eye forever as he walked from the surf at Hina. He was smiling, one hand was raised to push his water-darkened hair back from his face, and she remembered suddenly how he'd posed for the camera, how his laughter had changed to something else when he took her in his arms. She remembered the sun-heated smell of his skin, the water-slicked feel of his mouth on hers.

"I love you, Whitney," he'd whispered that day, and she, pathetic little fool that she was, she had believed him...

"*Aloha*, Whitney. Welcome home, my dear."

The snapshot fell from her fingers as she spun toward the door.

"Father." Her throat closed, and she swallowed dryly.

Her father smiled. "You looked as if you were a million miles away."

Her glance went to the snapshot lying at her feet. She bent, plucked it from the carpet, and tucked it into her pocket.

"I was," she said, gaining control of herself. "How have you been, Father?"

"Fine," he said, but Whitney's mind was clicking and whirring. He was lying, she thought, they'd all been lying. He was ill, anybody could tell that. She hadn't seen him since the last time he'd been in Los Angeles six months ago, and she remembered thinking then that he'd looked tired—but that had been nothing, compared to this. There were dark shadows under his eyes, deep grooves around his mouth.

"I'm sorry I couldn't be here to greet you." He stepped into the room and closed the door behind him. "But I had business elsewhere."

She nodded. "That's what Kichiro told me."

"Ah, did he? Good, good." There was a brief silence, and then her father cleared his throat. "How's the catering business?"

"It's been doing well. Father——"

"Clever idea, offering a week's worth of prepared meals to working women."

"So they tell me. Father——"

"I suppose you're wondering why I sent for you," her father said quickly.

"Yes. But—but I think I know."

J.T.'s eyes narrowed. "What do you mean? What the hell's Kichiro been telling you?"

"Nothing. He wouldn't say a word." Whitney ran her tongue along her lips. "You're ill, aren't you?"

Her father's bushy gray brows rose in surprise. "Ill? Where'd you ever get an idea like that?"

"Well, I put two and two together. I mean..."

"No," he said, shaking his head, "no, I'm not ill."

She felt a rush of relief. "Well, then," she said, "what's this all about?"

J.T. laughed. "No preliminaries, hmm? You just want to cut straight to the bottom line."

A flush rose into her cheeks. "Maybe that's because I had a good teacher."

Her father crossed the room and sank into the wing chair. "It's a long story," he said, ignoring the jibe. "I'm not quite sure where to start."

Whitney walked toward him. "At the beginning," she said quietly, as she sat down opposite him. "That's usually the best place, isn't it?"

He laughed politely. He's nervous, she thought in amazement. He's actually nervous.

"Well, then, let's see. I suppose you've noticed some changes in the house. Staffing changes, I mean."

"Yes. What happened? Did everybody quit at once?"

He leaned back and crossed his legs. "The place needs some sprucing up, too," he said, ignoring the question. He looked up and his eyes met hers. "I thought you might go into Honolulu with me next week and——"

"I won't be here next week," Whitney said quickly. "Didn't you get my message? I sent you a letter..."

"I know what you wrote, Whitney. You said you'd stay only the weekend. But that's out of the question."

She stared at him. Had he learned nothing in the past nine years? Surely he didn't think he could tell her what to do any more.

If he did, he was in for a rude awakening.

"I'm leaving the day after tomorrow, Father." Her voice was quiet but resolute. "I've arranged for the pilot who flew me in to pick me up Sunday afternoon." Whitney's brows rose. "And that reminds me—what happened to the Cessna? Doesn't Kenny work for you any more?"

J.T. grunted as he got to his feet. "We can talk about all this later," he said. "It's been a very long day, and I'm tired. We bought a new stud at auction a couple of months ago, and he hasn't been settling in well. I spent the morning with the vet . . ."

Whitney rose, too. "And you're deliberately evading my questions."

"I told you, I'm tired. I'll tell you everything, but first I'd like a shower and a change of clothes. I should think you'd want the same, after traveling all day." A forced smile spread across his face. "Why don't we meet in the library, in say, an hour? We can have some sherry, and——"

"Has all this something to do with the houses that are going up on the north meadow?"

The thought had only just come to her, but as the words left her mouth she knew, instinctively, that she was right.

Her father turned quickly and stared at her. All pretense had left his face. He looked as she remembered him best: cold, hard, and angry.

"That Kichiro's an old fool. Wait until I get hold of him. I specifically told him——"

"Kichiro didn't tell me anything. I told you that. It was me—I saw the fence, and I asked why it had been put up. Houses, he said, but he wouldn't say anything else."

J.T. scowled. "He'd damned well better not if he knows what's good for him."

"Is it true? Is someone building on Turner land? Did you sell off the meadow?"

Her father's brows drew together. "Everything later," he said sharply. He glanced at the Rolex on his wrist. "We're down to forty-five minutes, Whitney. Shower, change, and meet me in the study."

She laughed mirthlessly. "Just like old times. Everything according to Turner rules. Forty-five minutes. Not an hour, not half an hour..."

"My guest will be here soon. So if you insist on answers you'll either play by the rules or remain ignorant."

She looked at him in surprise. "Company? Tonight?"

"Yes. I know it's short notice..."

"Short notice?" Whitney shook her head. "I'm tired—you just said yourself, I've been traveling all day. And—and..."

And it's my first night home, she almost added, it's the first time I've been home in years—but what would be the point? Her father hadn't changed, and she hadn't expected him to. Still, it would have been nice to think, even for a little while, that he was happy to have her here.

"This is business, Whitney."

"Ah," she said, hating the disappointment that twisted through her, "of course. That explains it all. Business always comes first. If there's money to be made..."

Her father spun toward her, his face flushed. His voice was rough, almost harsh with anger.

"All right, you want this the hard way, that's how you'll get it. There's no Cessna because it costs too much to maintain. The servants have gone because their wages are a month late."

"What? I don't under——"

"And yes," he said, talking over her voice, "I sold part of the north meadow." He laughed humorlessly.

"Well, I didn't exactly sell it; let's just say the bank snatched it—just as they'll snatch every other acre of the ranch if I don't get my hands on enough money to keep them off my back." He drew a rasping breath. "Satisfied, Whitney? Now you have all the answers."

Whitney's legs were trembling. She sank down on the edge of her bed and stared at him blankly.

"What happened? How could all this have——?"

J.T. threw up his hands. "Never mind that. You wanted to cut to the bottom line, remember? Well, the bottom line is that we're going to lose everything—unless I can turn things around quickly."

She stared at him while she tried to make sense of what he'd just said. But she couldn't; the ranch—and her father's other interests—were worth millions. Tens of millions. How could he have jeopardized it all?

"I suppose you're wondering what all this has to do with you."

She drew a ragged breath. "Yes. I mean—I love this land. But there's nothing I can do to help, Father. I don't know anything about——"

"Appearances," her father said quickly. She looked up, and he nodded his head as if he'd just said something magical. "Show, my dear. That's what counts. The local bankers have given up on me. They know too much about me and the ranch. I had Collins from the First National out here for a wild goat hunt a couple of weeks ago, and the old bastard didn't miss a thing. 'Where's your cook, Turner?' he said. 'And your Van Gogh—don't tell me you sold it?'" —

Whitney shook her head. "The Van Gogh?"

"A basic fact of financial life is that the only time you can borrow money is when you don't need it."

"That doesn't make sense."

J.T. laughed. "No, of course it doesn't. But that's the way it is. Bankers don't run charities." He drew in his breath, then puffed it out. "I had to beat the bushes to find a source for the capital we need."

We, she thought. He was talking about her as if she were part of this. But she wasn't; she had never had anything to do with the Turner business interests. And she knew nothing about finance, not on this level. What could she possibly do that a J.T. Turner could not?

It was as if her father had read her mind. He walked quickly toward her and squatted down before her.

"A little diversion, Whitney, that's what we need. Something like tonight's dinner party. Good wine, good food, pleasant chatter. You, at the table, acting as my hostess—we can give the illusion that there's nothing wrong, no matter what anybody says."

Whitney's head was spinning. "You mean, you asked me here so I could entertain some banker? Father, that's—that's crazy. It's——"

"The man joining us tonight isn't a banker." Her father rose slowly and looked down at her. "But he has the money, and the facilities, to save us."

"What is he, then? A financier?"

J.T. laughed mirthlessly. "Some call him that. Actually, he's a shark who steps in when the scent of corporate blood is in the water."

"And you're turning to someone like that for help?"

"There's no one else. Believe me, if there were..."

Whitney got to her feet. "If he's what you say, then he won't be fooled for a minute by good wine or food or conversation."

"No," J.T.'s voice was cold. "No, he probably won't be. But he will be diverted. I'm certain of that. It was his suggestion, you see."

"His suggestion?" Whitney's brows rose. "What are you talking about?"

"He specifically asked that you be here." Her father's nostrils flared with distaste. "I had no choice, of course; I had to assure him that you would."

She stared at him, baffled. "Why would he ask that?" she said. "This man—what did you say his name was?"

"Alexander Baron," J.T. said, spitting the words as if they were venom.

Whitney touched her tongue to her lips. "Alexander Baron," she repeated softly. "Yes, I seem to... I've heard of him somewhere. Isn't he from the mainland? Something to do with corporate take-overs and venture capital?"

J.T. nodded. "In San Francisco. Yes, that's him." He frowned as he glanced at the gold Rolex glinting on his wrist. "And he's due here in less than an hour, for God's sake. Get moving, Whitney. We're dressing for dinner, of course."

Bewildered, she shook her head. "I didn't bring any long dresses with me. I didn't expect——"

"Your clothing's still in the closet. There must be something that will suit. I've had your mother's pearls put in your jewelry box. Wear them—they should add just the right touch."

"But why would Baron insist on meeting me?"

Her father paused in the doorway. His eyes narrowed, focused on her face, then slipped away.

"He knows you, Whitney." He cleared his throat, and she saw an uncharacteristic look of discomfort settle on his patrician features. "You and he have met before."

Whitney laughed and shook her head. "My business may be doing well, Father, but it doesn't put me in the company of venture capitalists."

"Baron spent his youth traveling the globe," J.T. said, as if she hadn't spoken. "'Learning about the world,' is how *Time* put it. I'd say that bumming from place to place, living on the largesse of others, is a more accurate description.''

''Yes. But——''

J.T.'s eyes fixed on her face. ''He worked his way across the South Pacific. From Australia to New Zealand, then to Tahiti. And then to Hawaii.''

There was something in the way her father was watching her—it was the way a cat watched a mouse, she thought suddenly, and a chill tiptoed along her spine.

''I still don't see——''

Her father sighed. ''He called himself 'Andy' when we knew him, my dear.''

She stared at him, horrified. No, she thought, no, it wasn't possible. It couldn't be.

But the grim expression on her father's face said that it could.

''It's only for one evening,'' her father said quickly. ''I know it's a great deal to ask, but——''

Whitney swung away. ''No.'' Her voice was sharp. ''It's out of the question.''

Her father strode toward her. His hands clasped her shoulders tightly.

''The bastard wants to make us eat crow,'' he said. ''But we can turn the tables on him, Whitney. We can show him that his money can't buy him the status to which Turners are born.''

Whitney shook her head. ''This is impossible,'' she whispered.

His fingers dug into her flesh as he spun her toward him. ''Are we to lose everything because of your foolish pride?''

She drew a deep breath. ''Father, please...''

Her father let go of her. ''I'll expect you in the library in forty-five minutes,'' he said, walking rapidly to the door.

''Father...''

"Forty-five minutes," he repeated firmly, and, before she could respond, the door closed quietly after him.

Whitney sank down on the bed. It wasn't possible. How could Alexander Baron and the boy who had taken her love, and left in its place a hatred so dark it had changed the course of her life, be the same person?

It was like a joke—except no one was laughing.

CHAPTER TWO

SHE had been sixteen that long-ago summer, the only girl in her class at Miss Porter's Academy who was really looking forward to summer vacation.

They were at the age when a holiday with one's family seemed a fate worse than death.

Allie was going to Europe with her parents. "Can you imagine?" she said, rolling her eyes to the ceiling, "two whole months of gawking at museums and churches. I'll die! I just know I'll die!"

Janet's folks were taking her on a tour of the mainland. "I'll go crazy first," she promised. "My father's got all these routes planned out—we're going to drive about a zillion miles. How will I live through it?"

Iris was to spend the summer cruising the South Pacific on her father's yacht. "He says it'll be the educational experience of a lifetime," she moaned. "And he bought me a globe—a globe, can you believe it?"

All eyes turned to Whitney. "You're so lucky," Iris said, summing up everybody's feelings. "Your father treats you like a grown-up, Whitney. He never drags you around with him when you'd rather be doing something else, does he?"

Whitney smiled and said no, he didn't. What she didn't add was that her father never took her anywhere. It wasn't that he didn't travel. He did, a lot. But it was all business connected, and he never thought of asking her to join him.

Sometimes, in her darker moments, she wondered if he ever thought of her at all, but then she reminded herself that her father had a far-flung empire to run. He loved her, she knew he did. It was just that he was very busy.

Early that summer, just after her vacation began, J.T. sprained his ankle. It wasn't serious, but it kept him housebound for a couple of weeks—just long enough for Whitney's dream to come true.

For the first time ever, her father noticed her.

But her joy was short-lived. In no time at all, he made it clear that he wasn't pleased with what he'd seen. Whitney was almost an adult now, he said, but she was not the proper young woman he had hoped her to be. She was too much a tomboy. She didn't dress properly. And she certainly wasn't behaving appropriately.

The summer Whitney had so looked forward to closed around her like a prison as J.T. laid down the rules she was to live by.

She was to stop hanging around at the stables. She was to remember that she was a Turner in her dealings with the ranch hands. She was to be measured for business suits that would replace the jeans and T-shirts she'd always worn around the ranch. She was to appear at the formal dinners J.T. held from time to time and learn to be a proper hostess to his guests.

She was, in short, to behave in ways that befitted her status as her father's daughter.

By the time midsummer came, Whitney was miserable. She hated this new existence, but she had been raised to be an obedient daughter. She told herself that things would change as soon as J.T. was back on his feet. Once he picked up the reins of his life again, he would forget about her, just as he had in the past.

And that was exactly what happened. She awoke one morning to find him gone. Emma, the newest in an endless procession of housekeepers, said J.T. had left by helicopter just after dawn, called away to somewhere or other on urgent business. He would phone or cable; his lawyers would know where to reach him in the event of an emergency; he would see Whitney in a few weeks...

Blah, blah, blah, Whitney thought, although her expression was properly attentive.

For the first time in her life, her father's callousness didn't hurt her. Instead, she felt as if she had been set free.

Within minutes, she peeled off the custom-made trouser suit and exchanged it for faded jeans and an old T-shirt. Then she hurried down to the stables to groom the little roan mare that had been hers since her tenth birthday. She had not done so all summer.

"Your job is to ride her," J.T. had said. "I pay stable hands to curry the animals."

If the hands were surprised to see her, they didn't let her know it. She was greeted as she'd been before the start of the summer, with pleasant smiles and no special treatment, and after a few minutes she felt as if she'd never been away.

She might be "Miss Whitney" when her father returned in a few weeks. But for now, with dirt on her nose and straw in her hair, she was the young woman she'd always been.

That was how she looked the day she met Alex Baron. Of course, he hadn't called himself by that name then. He was "Andy"—that was how he'd introduced himself.

She was alone in the stable, mucking out the mare's stall, knee deep in hay, when the door swung open. She looked up, squinting against the bright flare of sunlight. There was a figure in the doorway—a man or a boy, she really couldn't see anything more than his outline.

"Hey, there," he said, "is the *luna* around?"

Whitney straightened up, still holding the pitchfork in one hand.

"The foreman? His office is out back."

"I checked," he said, stepping forward a little. "Nobody's there."

She could see him more clearly now, with his body blocking off the light. The stranger was a young man wearing faded jeans, like hers, and a cotton T-shirt with the word "Turner" on it, also like hers. But the sleeves had been cut out of his, exposing well-muscled, tanned arms.

"Where else would he be?" he said. "Do you know?"

"No," she said, "I—I..."

Her words faded away while her gaze swept over him. She had never seen anyone like him before. Part of it was the way he held himself, and part of it was the way he looked. He was—he was very masculine, despite the sun-streaked hair that hung almost to his shoulders. Her father would frown and say he looked like a bum, but he didn't. He looked—he looked...

Whitney felt a funny tingle run through her. All at once, she was painfully conscious of her smudged cheeks and the bits of hay caught in her hair.

The sensation was a new one for a girl who never cared how she looked, unless she was making a command appearance at J.T.'s dinner table. It made her feel somehow shy. Their eyes met; she thought she saw laughter glinting in his.

Whitney became completely flustered. She compensated for it by—for the first time in her life—hiding behind the imperious demeanour of a Turner.

"Perhaps I can help you," she said, drawing herself up and giving him a cool little smile.

He grinned. "I doubt it."

She felt a flush rising in her cheeks. "I think you'd better tell me what it is you want."

She almost cringed at the way she sounded. What was wrong with her? Her father spoke to people like that, not she. Whitney took a step forward, but before she could offer an apology the boy swept an imaginary cap from his head and made her a low, sweeping bow.

"Certainly, my lady. Would my lady be so kind as to tell me where to unload a truckload of feed sacks?"

He *was* laughing at her; she could hear it in his teasing retort. Whitney flushed, stabbed the pitchfork into the hay, and put her hands on her hips.

"Do you have any idea who I am?" she demanded.

"Uh-huh." His expression grew deadpan, and his glance flickered to her feet, then back to her face. "You're a Lady—up to her ankles in manure."

Her glance followed his. She looked up quickly, determined not to give ground. But he was smiling, and his smile was infectious. After a second or two, she began to smile, too.

He was just a boy after all. He'd caught her by surprise; that was why she'd acted so strangely. And it was silly.

"Tell you what," she said, wiping her hands on her denim-clad backside, "give me a minute to finish here, and I'll find you a place to unload those sacks."

"Done," he said, "but only if you let me give you a hand first."

Whitney shrugged her shoulders. "Sure. Why not?"

They worked in companionable silence until the stall was clean and laid with fresh hay, and then Whitney followed him outside to where he'd left a pickup truck bearing the Turner logo.

"You can unload around the side there," she said. "I'll help you."

"The sacks are heavy," he warned, but Whitney tossed her head.

"Don't be such a male chauvinist," she said. "I'm stronger than you think."

She almost staggered under the weight of the first sack, but she wouldn't admit it, although by the time they'd emptied the truck her arms and back were aching. But it didn't matter; what counted was that she was having fun. The stranger had a nice sense of humor: it took a while to get the truck unloaded, but it seemed like just minutes because he had her laughing and smiling all the while.

When they finished, he wiped his hand on his jeans-clad leg and held it out to her.

"Thanks a lot." He paused, and a boyish grin tugged at the corners of his mouth. "We haven't even introduced ourselves to each other. I'm Andy."

"Whitney," she said, putting her hand in his.

Months later, she would remember that something had seemed to flicker in his eyes.

"Whitney Turner?"

"Yes," she answered, and, perhaps because her father had made her terribly self-conscious about who she was this summer, she lifted her chin almost defiantly. "Does it matter?"

"No," he said immediately, "of course it doesn't."

There was a silence, and then Andy drew back his hand. "Well," he said, "thanks again."

He turned away, and suddenly Whitney took a step forward. "Would you—would you like some lemonade?"

He gave her a dazzling smile. "Sure. I'd love some."

That was the start of their friendship. They spent the afternoon together that first day, talking about anything and everything, until finally Andy said if he didn't get back to work he'd probably lose his job.

For the second time in her life, Whitney spoke like a Turner.

"I wouldn't let them fire you," she said.

Andy's smile cooled. "What makes you think I'd let you intervene? Do you really think I'd ask for special treatment?"

She didn't, especially as the summer wore on and she got to know him better. Andy was independent; he was used to relying on no one but himself. It had given him a toughness that was in vivid contrast to the other boys she knew. Sons of her father's friends or brothers of her school chums, they all came off second best when she compared them to Andy.

He'd worked his way across the Pacific, he'd had all kinds of jobs, and even though she knew there was nothing romantic or exciting about packing bananas or loading freighters his stories made those things sound almost intriguing. He had been on his own for years, apparently—he never mentioned family at all. He was only twenty, but he'd already done and seen everything. In fact, it was that more than anything else that made Whitney lie to him about her age. She was eighteen, she told him, afraid Andy might look on her as a child if he knew the truth.

But that was the only untruth she told him. She was open and honest with him in every other way. He was the first real friend she'd ever had, the first person she'd felt completely relaxed with—and then, in August, their friendship ignited into something else.

The offshore wind pushed a hot, muggy day before it, the kind that was rare in the islands. Andy had the afternoon off, and they were sitting in the shade of an Ohia tree, down by the stables, enduring the humidity.

But it was impossible. The heat was too intense. For a moment, Whitney was tempted to suggest a swim in the pool behind the house. But her father was due home later in the day, and she knew it wouldn't be wise to let him see her with Andy. In fact, lately she'd worried quite a lot about how she'd go on seeing her new friend, once J.T. was back.

There had to be a cool place they could go together, she thought—and all at once, a name came to her.

"Kahuna Gorge," she said happily. "Why didn't I think of it sooner?"

Andy looked at her. "Kahuna Gorge? What's that?"

"An air-conditioned paradise. How'd you like to go there?"

"You're dreaming. Nothing's air-conditioned on this island, except the big hotels." He wiped the sweat from his brow with his forearm. "Haven't you read the stuff the Chamber of Commerce puts out? You don't need air-conditioning in Hawaii."

Whitney got to her feet. "Well, they're right. All you need to know is how to get out of the sun." She gave him a smug smile. "I'll get us a thermos of iced tea while you saddle the horses."

"The lady's hallucinating," Andy said, groaning as he stood up.

But he did as she'd asked and, an hour later, they were at the Gorge.

Whitney had been right, it was much cooler here. There was always a breeze blowing in from the sea; besides, the thick trees that grew on the lip of the ravine gave shade from even the most piercing of the sun's rays.

They sprawled in the lush grass, munching on crackers and fruit, passing the thermos back and forth, and talking. Suddenly, the sky turned dark. Whitney had seen it happen before: she grabbed Andy's hand and they raced for the trees, but it was too late. The clouds opened up, and cool rain poured down in a torrent. Within seconds, they were drenched.

The rain stopped as abruptly as it had started, but by then Whitney was shaking.

"Are you okay?" Andy said.

She nodded. "F-f-fine," she answered, her teeth dancing together like castanets.

Andy put his arm around her and drew her into the heat of his body. He had never touched her before, except by accident, and now she was assailed by a thousand sensations. She could feel the hardness of his encircling arm, the dampness of his shirt, the sun-warmed smell of his skin.

A tremor went through her, a tremor Andy misinterpreted. At least, that was what she thought at the time. Later, Whitney knew that he deliberately acted as if he didn't know what was happening to her.

"You're freezing," he said, and before she could protest he stripped off his shirt and wrapped it around her shoulders.

Her heart skipped a beat as his hands moved across hers. "Andy..."

"Don't argue," he said. "You'll catch a chill."

"I won't. And you need your shirt. Without it..."

Without it, he was half-naked. Her words trailed away, and color rose in her cheeks as she stared at him. Andy's skin was golden in color, like the summer grass in the north meadow. There was a thatch of hair across his chest where dampness glinted like diamonds.

Her throat felt as if it were closing. "Andy," she said, and at that very moment he reached out and began to button his shirt closed around her.

Her breath caught as his hand brushed lightly across her breasts. She felt her entire body strain toward his; a sound that was part whimper, part moan, broke from her lips.

Andy's hands stilled. "Whitney?" he said softly.

She whispered his name, and then they were in each other's arms, kissing with a passion that she, in her innocence, had never even imagined.

Even now, nine years later, Whitney could remember the heat of that first embrace. Standing in her pink and white bedroom, she closed her eyes and recalled the rain-slicked feel of Andy's skin beneath her trembling fingers;

the scent of his body as he drew her down into the soft grass; the feel of his mouth as it took hers.

Whitney put her hands to her face. The bastard had been so clever. He'd planned everything, right down to the last detail. She'd wondered, for a long time after, why he hadn't taken her that day. God knew he could have: by the time he'd finished kissing her, she'd been dizzy with wanting him.

But she'd finally figured it out. He wasn't ready to take things that far, not that afternoon. He'd needed a better setting and a guaranteed audience before going to the next step of his ugly little scheme.

He'd put her from him, carefully, as if she were so fragile she might shatter in his hands. And he had put her from him each time they were together over the next couple of weeks, until finally, as she knew he'd planned, Whitney had been aching for his possession.

With the innocence of her sixteen years, she'd thought she loved him, thought he loved her, too. Perhaps that was what had made that last day so especially humiliating and painful.

The day had begun badly. Word had come that her father, away on yet another trip, was coming home the next evening. He would stay a month this time, which meant Whitney would be under close scrutiny again.

The prospect had filled her with despair, and she tried to forget what lay ahead. She'd been with Andy as the sun dipped toward the sea, lying in his arms in the stable, on a bed of sweet smelling hay, almost dizzy with awareness of his hard, aroused body. He wanted her—not even the clothing separating them could hide it.

He had begun kissing her, over and over, until finally she was moving against him, blind to everything but the urgency of her need.

Her plea had been wordless, but her body had spoken insistently. And Andy—Andy had muttered something, clasped her to him so tightly she could barely breathe, then said he couldn't go on this way any more. It was time, he'd said. He had to have her.

Whitney walked to the window and stared out blindly. Night had fallen; she had almost forgotten how swiftly darkness surrounded you in the islands.

It had surrounded them that night, settling over them like black velvet.

Her arms had twined around Andy's neck. "Then take me," she'd whispered.

Gently, he'd clasped her wrists and brought her hands to her sides.

Not here, he said thickly. Not in the barn. And not in any of the places that were their own, Kahuna Gorge or Hina Beach, where he'd first touched her breasts and made her cry out with passion.

He would come to her in her room that night, he'd said, and make love to her properly, on clean sheets in a soft bed, and they would spend the night in each other's arms.

Whitney's heart had raced with excitement. At first the risks had seemed enormous, but gradually they'd begun to diminish. What could go wrong? Her father would be away until tomorrow. As for Emma, she would tell her she had a headache and was going to bed early.

After tonight, who knew how long it would be until they were alone again?

"Leave your *lanai* door unlocked," Andy had whispered, "and I'll come to you."

In the dark, Whitney had waited, trembling, for the sound of his footsteps on the balcony. By the time he'd arrived, she was terrified. Of him, of herself—of what they were about to do.

"I've changed my mind," she'd said, by way of greeting, and clever Andy—smiled and said that was okay with him, he'd had second thoughts, too.

"Just let me hold you in my arms," he'd whispered, and he did. But after a while he'd begun kissing her and touching her, and soon her fear had fled, passion blooming darkly in its place.

Whitney turned away from the window and put her knuckles to her mouth. She'd never even heard her father's footsteps on the stairs, nor his knock. She'd never heard the door opening—the first awareness she'd had of anything but Andy's arms and his kisses was when light had flooded the room.

"Whitney!" her father had roared. There'd been a stunned moment of silence, and then J.T. had pointed to the door. "Go to my rooms and wait there."

How many times, over the years, had she wondered what would have happened if she hadn't obeyed? What would Andy have done if she'd insisted on staying with him to face her father's wrath?

It didn't matter. She *had* obeyed; she was only sixteen, and she'd been a dutiful daughter all her life. Sometimes, remembering, she thought Andy had called after her, even though she knew he hadn't. It was just a trick her mind played, an extra cruelty added to all the rest.

She'd waited, trembling, for more than an hour, and then her father had appeared, his face dark and frozen with distaste.

"How could you?" he said coldly. "My daughter, with a boy like that."

"You don't understand. Andy loves me."

She staggered back as her father's open hand slammed against her cheek.

"You pathetic little fool. He *used* you. And now he's gone."

"You sent him away?" Whitney tried to shoulder past him, but her father caught her by the shoulders and shook her.

"Listen to me," he growled. "He used you, from start to finish."

She shook her head and clapped her hands to her ears. "You're lying."

But her father kept talking, his voice cold and deliberate, until finally the whole malignant story was out, lying between them like something coiled and evil.

Andy had been clever and observant. He'd seen how innocent and naïve she was, and made his plans accordingly. He'd set out to seduce her, holding off only until he could be certain he'd found a time and place when they were sure to be discovered by J.T. himself.

Whitney refused to believe it. "It's a lie! He didn't even know you were coming home tonight."

But he *had* known, J.T. said grimly. Andy had been with Kenny, the helicopter pilot, when arrangements had been made for Kenny to pick her father up and return him this evening instead of tomorrow.

"He *knew* I'd be back tonight, Whitney, just as he knew I'd come to your room to check on you once Emma told me you were ill."

"But—but why?" she'd sobbed. "Why would he have done all that?"

"Because he hates us."

"I don't understand."

J.T. smiled grimly. "The boy's uneducated. He has no future. But, instead of admitting that to himself, he'd rather despise people like us for our money."

Whitney shook her head. "No. No, we talked about money. Andy didn't..."

"Didn't he? Your little indiscretion just cost me twenty-five thousand dollars. That's what that—that stable boy demanded in return for his promise to leave the islands."

Whitney stared at him. "No," she whispered. "You— you got rid of him—you did something..."

"Yes," her father said, his mouth grim. "I certainly did. I met the bastard's price."

When she realized he was telling her the truth, she went pale.

"He made a fool of me," she whispered.

J.T.'s mouth narrowed. "He made fools of the both of us. But I salvaged our pride. I told him—well, it doesn't matter. What matters is that he's gone. In a week or two, this whole incident will be forgotten."

But it wasn't. In fact, nothing was the same after that. There was a new housekeeper in Emma's place the next morning.

"If she'd been doing her job, the boy would never have gotten into your good graces," J.T. growled.

Even the ranch she had once loved seemed different. Whitney had taken Andy to all her special places, and now they seemed defiled.

Within the year, she'd asked to be sent away to school, and her father had agreed.

"But you will return to the ranch after you've graduated," he'd warned. "Your place is here, on Turner land."

She hadn't returned, though, despite his insistence. What had happened to her that night had changed her forever. It had left her embittered, but it had given her a new strength.

She couldn't live the life her father had planned for her, and after a year on the mainland she'd found the courage to tell him so.

Eventually, her father had given up asking, and they'd settled into a relationship no more distant than the one they'd always had, except that now they were separated physically as well as emotionally.

Somewhere in the darkness, a night bird shrilled its cry. Whitney shuddered, then turned her back to the window. Remembering had been painful, but it had given her the courage she needed to face what lay ahead.

She felt in control of herself again.

Her life was hers to live, not her father's, not Alexander Baron's.

And she was damned if she was going to let either one of them use her.

CHAPTER THREE

WHITNEY strode from lamp to lamp, switching on the lights until the bedroom was a shimmering beacon against the darkness.

Incredible, she thought. Impossible! To think that her father had brought her all this distance to be part of this—this charade!

It wasn't as if she had any illusions about J.T. She had seen him destroy friendships in the name of revenge, violate ethics in the name of gain. She knew he had always put his own interests, and those of Turner Enterprises, ahead of everything, and everyone, else.

But what he'd planned now went beyond anything she'd ever imagined him capable of. God! Did he have no feelings for her at all? She was his daughter, not just some stranger he needed to bait his trap. J.T. knew, better than anyone, how close she'd come to being destroyed by Alexander Baron years ago.

Her mouth twisted as she pulled her jacket from the closet and thrust her arms into the sleeves. As for Baron himself—damn the man for his arrogance! He had used her once; did he really think she'd let him use her again?

Whitney drew a deep breath. The hows and whys of it didn't matter, she thought as she hoisted her suitcase from the floor. What counted was that both men had underestimated her. She'd been little more than a child nine years ago, driven by newly awakened sexual desire and far too young to take charge of her life.

Now she was a woman. And she would protect herself, even if no one else did.

She was trembling as she gathered her things together. If only Kenny were still here, flying the Turner 'copter. As it was, she'd have to find another way off the ranch. It would take too long to phone for a light plane or a helicopter, then wait for its arrival. Baron would be here long before it arrived.

Well, she would take a Jeep or a Range Rover from the sprawling outbuildings behind the house and head for the nearest public highway. The ranch was huge—it covered seventy-five thousand acres—and there were always rugged vehicles available for whomever needed one.

Whitney looped her shoulder bag over her arm and hoisted her suitcase. She'd drive to the nearest public road, then to the airport at Keahole, and then she'd take the first plane back to the mainland and to hell with her father and the ranch and the stupidly sentimental feelings that had come over her when she'd laid eyes on both of them.

You can't go home again, somebody had said, and Whitney only wished she had believed it. She grimaced as she opened the bedroom door and stepped out into the hall. Why hadn't she demanded answers before she'd agreed to come back? She should have insisted on being told exactly why her father wanted to see her instead of letting her imagination convince her he was ill or in some desperate need . . .

The doorbell pealed as she reached the top of the stairs. Her heart gave a little lurch and she hesitated. Forty-five minutes, her father had said. Surely the time hadn't passed yet?

She peered over the banister, watching as the housekeeper walked to the front door. She couldn't see it from where she stood, but she could hear it swing open, hear voices—the housekeeper's and another, assuredly masculine—and then the door closed.

Footsteps rang against the slate floor, and Whitney shrank back into the shadows on the landing.

"If you'll wait just a moment, sir, I'll announce you to Mr. Turner," she heard the housekeeper say.

"Thank you."

Whitney's breath caught. The voice was deeper, harsher—but she would have recognized it in her sleep.

Alexander Baron had arrived.

Just get going, a little voice inside her whispered. Go down the back stairs and through the kitchen and straight out of the door. He'll never see you, he'll never know...

But her legs wouldn't move. She felt paralyzed, like one of the butterflies in the display cases that lined the library walls. She had always hated going into that room when she was little. It had seemed wrong that creatures so free and beautiful should be impaled against the black velvet, important only as specimens in a collection.

"Baron." Her father's voice was hearty and just a shade too loud. "How was your flight? I'd have sent my man to pick you up at the airport, but our 'copter is out for servicing."

"Really?"

One word, Whitney thought, only one word. But it was filled with contemptuous amusement.

"Well," her father said briskly, "what can I get you to drink? Irish whiskey, perhaps? Bourbon? I have a case of Wild Turkey that——"

Again, there was that swift, singular response. "Vodka."

"Vodka?" J.T.'s voice grew unctuous, as if Baron had requested something as banal as a soft drink. Whitney could almost see the amused little smile she knew would be on his face. "Certainly, if you insist. Are you sure I can't tempt you with something else? A friend in Glasgow sent me a single malt Scotch from his own distillery—he produces only a few hundred cases a year, and——"

"Vodka," Baron repeated. "Stolichnaya Cristal."

There was the barest pause. "Yes, of course. I'm sure we——"

"I would prefer it chilled."

"Chilled." There was another hesitation. "Yes," J.T. said. "Certainly." And now there was something in his voice Whitney had never heard before. "I'll tell my housekeeper to——"

"Straight up, with a slice of lime."

"Of course. I'm sure we can——"

Baron's voice sliced through her father's. "Where is your daughter, Turner?"

"My daughter. Whitney is—she'll be down shortly."

"Will she?" There it was again, that amused disdain. "I thought perhaps she'd have begged off this evening."

"No," J.T. said quickly, "no, she's—she's looking forward to seeing you again."

Whitney closed her eyes. Father, she thought, how could you?

"But I thought," her father went on, "that, while we waited, we might step into my study." His voice gained strength, the tone growing intimate. Whitney could envisage him stepping closer to his guest, perhaps putting his arm loosely around the other man's shoulders, giving him the little smile that mocked as much as it offered friendship. "*Time* mentioned your interest in primitive sculptures, and, of course, I've one of the world's finest collections of——"

Baron cut his speech short. "The one you're planning to sell next month at Sotheby's?" He laughed in a way that made clear his opinion of the pieces. "Sorry, Turner, but I'm not interested."

"No. No, that's not what I meant, Baron. I only thought—— "

"What I want to see are the papers I requested."

J.T. cleared his throat. "Of course. But I thought we'd wait until after——"

"Now."

Her father made a muffled sound Whitney knew was meant to be a chuckle. An unexpected twinge of compassion rose in her breast.

"I've always thought it best," he said, "to break bread with a man before——"

"What you've always thought," Baron said in chilled tones, "has no bearing on anything. Now, have you the papers or haven't you?"

Whitney held her breath, waiting. Surely her father would throw the man out now. Surely...

"Yes." J.T.'s voice was papery. "Certainly. If you'll just come this way..."

Footsteps clattered across the floor. A door opened, then closed, and Whitney sagged back against the wall.

Of all that had happened today, nothing was as shocking as the scene that had just been played out on the floor below.

"We can show him that his money can't buy him the status to which Turners are born." She could hear her father's words in her mind.

She knew what J.T. had intended. He had always been a master at subtle intimidation. Whitney had seen him do it a hundred times. He was the impeccable host, and who could fault him if whatever he offered his guests just happened to be finer than anything they could ever afford?

But it looked as if her father had misjudged the enemy. Subtlety didn't mean a damn to a man like Alexander Baron, and why should it? The game he'd played with her years ago hadn't been subtle at all, it had been brazen and ugly and deliberate—just as his treatment of her father had been ever since he'd walked into the house this evening.

Carefully, she moved back along the landing to her room, opened the door, and slipped inside. How could her father have been such a fool? He should have known the kind of man he'd be up against. After all, J.T. had been there when Alexander Baron had taken his first brutal step up the ladder. He hadn't even tried to stop him.

A knock sounded at the door and she started. "Who is it?"

The door opened a crack and the housekeeper peered at her. "Your father asks you to please come down to dinner, miss."

Whitney drew a breath. "What's your name, please?"

"Pearl, miss."

"Pearl." She swallowed. "Pearl, please tell my father that I—that I..."

The housekeeper had no trouble interpreting her hesitancy.

"Your father says you must do it, miss," she said in a whisper that made conspirators of them both.

"No," Whitney said quickly.

She fell silent, while Alex's mocking voice echoed in her head. *I thought perhaps she'd have begged off this evening*, he'd said—and suddenly Whitney knew that her father was right. She did have to go downstairs, not because he was demanding it, but because Alexander Baron was so certain that she would not.

It wasn't her father who'd orchestrated the evening, it was Baron. J.T. was only a minor player—even he must see that now. Baron had planned everything, just as he had done all those years ago when he'd parlayed a liaison with the boss's naïve daughter into a twenty-five-thousand-dollar stake. He'd expected her to hide in her room, just as he'd expected J.T. to play lord of the manor.

How he must be laughing! It wasn't everybody who got to make fools of the Turners twice in a lifetime.

"Miss?"

Whitney looked up. "All right," she said quickly. "Tell my father—tell him I'll be down in a few minutes."

Her heart pounded as she shut the door and leaned back against it.

"We can show him that his money can't buy him the status to which Turners are born."

If only she believed in that nonsense, the way her father did.

But you didn't have to believe something to carry it off, did you? The disdain she felt for Alexander Baron was real enough. As for the rest—all she needed was the proper gown, the cool splendor of her mother's pearls, and the sophisticated little tricks she'd watched her father practice on the less fortunate for years.

She could do it. She *had* to do it. At least then she might play tonight's match to a draw.

It was small recompense for what Alexander Baron had done to her.

But it would have to suffice.

The grandfather clock on the landing, the one Great-great-grandfather Turner had brought with him on the whaler from Boston, chimed the half hour as Whitney stepped from her room and quietly closed the door after her. It had taken quite a bit more than a few minutes to dress, but then ladies of the manor almost always made dramatic entrances. And this entrance would surely be just that.

She took a deep breath. Her palms were damp and her stomach was in knots as she started slowly down the stairs.

Be calm, she told herself. Don't let what you're feeling show. Alexander Baron might be a lot of things, but he was never a fool.

Outwardly, she looked just right for the part she was to play. A last, long look in the mirror had assured her of that. It hadn't been easy—precious minutes had ticked by while she'd looked for something to wear. Her father had been right, all her old things were still in the closet. But she had left here a child and returned a woman, long past the age of pink and blue chiffon or demure eyelet cotton.

At the last second, when she'd almost given up hope, she'd come across a gown tucked away in the rear of the closet, a long column of ivory silk that had been bought for her seventeenth birthday party. There'd never been any party, of course—Whitney had left for boarding school on the mainland by then—but the gown was still there, and it was the closest she could find to something a grown woman would wear.

She'd attacked it ruthlessly with a pair of nail scissors. The little cape and mandarin collar were all of one piece and fell away easily, revealing a strapless bodice. She'd disposed of the pale blue sash at the waist with one snip, then opened the front-buttoning skirt from ankle to thigh so that a long length of tanned leg teased the eye when she moved.

When she finished, her creation was no threat to James Galanos or Oscar de la Renta. But it had the look of sophistication that she would need to get her through the next hours.

She swept her hair back from her temples and secured it with a pair of antique scrimshaw combs, then let the rest tumble to her shoulders in a straight silken fall. Ordinarily, she didn't use much makeup. But the ivory silk made her look pale and so she brushed layers of black mascara on her already dark lashes, whisked her cheekbones with dusky rose blusher, then coated her lips with pale pink gloss. Her hands trembled when she put her mother's pearl earrings in her lobes, trembled again when she closed the sapphire and diamond clasp of the matching choker and lay it carefully in the hollow of her throat.

At last, she had glanced into the mirror. The woman looking back at her was a cool, sophisticated stranger. No one would ever guess that her heart was lying like a lump of cold dough in her breast.

"Ready or not," she'd whispered with a shaky laugh, and she'd stepped from her bedroom into the hall.

Now, midway down the long staircase, her courage almost failed her. Male voices drifted up from the library, and her stomach clenched.

There was still time to fly up the steps, retreat to her room...

"Whitney." She looked down to where her father was standing alone at the bottom of the stairs. His usually ruddy face seemed pale, and there was a polite smile pasted on his mouth. "There you are, my dear. Mr. Baron and I were just beginning to wonder what was keeping you."

She swallowed. You're on, she thought, and from some inner well of strength she summoned an equally polite smile.

"I'm sorry, Father," she said. Her voice quavered a little, and she cleared her throat. "I hope I haven't kept you waiting very——"

"You did. But it was well worth it."

The voice was deep and commanding. Whitney's heart skipped a beat, but her expression gave nothing away as she looked toward the library.

Her heart turned over. The boy she had known was gone, and in his place was a man. A handsome, virile man, one she would never have recognized, not in a thousand years. The shoulder-length, honey-colored hair had been tamed, expensively cut so that it barely brushed the collar of his black dinner jacket. Baron had grown, too, or at least he had matured. The boy she remembered had been lean, but the man before her was broad shouldered and muscular.

She knew, instinctively, that he was far too male for anyone to ever call him by his childish nickname any more.

"Whitney?"

Her father's voice drew her back. She tore her eyes from Alexander Baron and made herself descend the last few steps. At the foot of the staircase she hesitated, her eyes going to the figure in the library doorway again.

Not everything about him had changed. His eyes, those pale, ice-blue eyes, were the same as they'd always been, still fringed with spiky lashes as thick and dark as her own. His skin was still golden in color, looking as if the sun had kissed it. And his mouth, that sculpted, hard mouth...

"Well?" His voice was a purr. "Do I pass muster?"

She blinked. His lips were curved in amusement. He was laughing at her, and no wonder. She had come down these stairs determined to dazzle him with her cool sophistication and instead she was gawking.

Color stained her cheeks, but she managed to incline her head a fraction of an inch in a gesture she knew would seem imperious.

"Mr. Baron," she said as she walked toward him. The evenness of her voice pleased her. "Welcome to the Turner Ranch. I'm sorry if I seemed to stare—I was trying to recall when we might have met."

She heard her father's quick intake of breath, saw Baron's brows rise. Score one for my team, Whitney thought grimly as she extended her hand.

A slight smile arced across his mouth. "Indeed?" His fingers closed around hers, hard and cool.

She hesitated, but only for a second. He was smiling, but his eyes were cold. Don't push too hard, he seemed to be saying, I know what you're doing.

He couldn't. But what was the point in rushing things? The evening was young. She didn't have to win the game just yet. Besides, the longer it took—the more points she accumulated—the sweeter the victory would be.

Whitney tossed her head back in a way that made her hair ripple across her shoulders.

"You do seem familiar," she said pleasantly. Her forehead furrowed a little. His hand was still clasping hers, the pressure of his fingers hard enough to be discomforting. "But, of course, it's been so long." She glanced at her father. "How many years ago did you say it was since Mr. Baron worked for us, Father? Nine? Ten?"

J.T. was watching her, a puzzled look in his eyes. "Nine," he said with precision. "Surely you remember, Whitney?"

She shrugged. "I'm afraid not."

Baron smiled. "Is that right?"

"There've been so many workers on the ranch over the years..." She gave him a dazzling smile. "I apologize. But I'm sure I'll place you before the night ends."

His smile changed, curled into something that sent a sudden chill along her flesh.

"Oh, you will, Miss Turner. You will."

She stared up at him, trying to see beyond the cool mask. His eyes were like opaque glass, dark and unreadable. Make some offer of contrition, however slight, she told herself—but something in the way he was watching her made her spine stiffen.

"We'll see," she said, her voice as soft and cool as his.

"Whitney." Her father's voice was sharp. She looked at him as he strode toward her. His face was flushed, and there was an angry warning in his eyes.

She smiled agreeably. "Yes, Father?"

"I'd like to speak to you for a moment." The smile he gave his guest was forced. "It occurs to me I never asked my daughter her preference in wines. Will you excuse us for a moment?"

Alexander Baron's hand tightened on hers, then fell away. "Of course," he said, letting go of her. "I'd like to wash up, if I may."

"Yes, of course. Just down that hall and to your right." J.T.'s smile fled as soon as Baron had disappeared down the corridor. "Dammit, Whitney," he hissed, "what are you trying to do?"

"Only what you asked of me, Father," she said calmly. "I'm reminding our guest that he doesn't belong here."

"But he does," her father said grimly. "I thought I explained all this to you, Whitney. He's my only hope. I need——"

"His money. Yes, so you said. But you also said you wanted to show him that not all the money in the world could make him equal to a Turner."

J.T. grimaced. "I meant it to be a subtle message, for God's sake. If you go on rubbing his nose in it the way you have, the man's liable to get up and walk out—and then what will I do?"

Whitney lifted her chin. "If you expect me to grovel, Father..."

"I expect you to use your head," her father said sharply. "I expect you to treat him politely, even if it's difficult."

"Difficult?" Whitney shrugged free of her father's grasp. "It's damned near impossible. You'll never convince me. That man has no right to be here."

"I hope I haven't kept you waiting." Whitney whirled around. Alexander Baron had come up silently behind her. His lips lifted in an easy smile. For a second, she thought he might even be laughing. "I'm sorry," he said pleasantly, looking from father to daughter. "Have I interrupted?" His smile broadened, until it was like a cat's. "What is it, Whitney? Is your father finding it difficult to convince you?"

She stared at him. "To convince me...?"

"About the wine." Their eyes met and held. "I'd listen to him, if I were you, Whitney—unless you want to see everything fall apart before it's even started."

Her father cleared his throat. "Baron, she didn't mean——"

Alexander Baron laughed softly. "Of course she did. No hostess wants to see a carefully planned meal start the wrong way. Isn't that right, Whitney?"

Whitney drew a deep breath. A dozen sharp responses whirled through her head. He was toying with them both, playing a game of nerves and semantics, and she wanted to tell him that it was a game he would not win.

But her tongue seemed stuck to the roof of her mouth. Her silence had to do with the fear she saw in her father's eyes, with the coldness she saw in Baron's—and it had to do with something else, something she dared not try and identify.

"Mr. Baron," she said finally, and he shook his head. "Alex."

His tone left no room for compromise. "Alex," she repeated, but then there didn't seem to be anything more to say. After a moment, he smiled and reached for her hand.

"Shall we go in to dinner?" he said, tucking her hand into the curve of his arm.

Before she could do anything about it, Whitney found herself being led to her own table.

"How'd the market do today?" she heard her father ask, and Baron answered, pleasantly enough.

And all the while, through the wine and food and coffee and liqueurs that followed, the only thing Whitney could think of was that Alexander Baron was not playing the game he'd been invited to play.

The game he *was* playing was strictly of his own devising.

And its rules were known only to him.

CHAPTER FOUR

"...And so then I said, 'Hell, Borden, what's the problem? If you want me to put up another fifty thousand dollars, just come out and say so.'" J.T. leaned across the snowy damask cloth and gave his guest a man-to-man smile. "So the damned fool looks me straight in the eye and says, 'Okay, Turner, I want you to put up another fifty thou.'" J.T. grinned. "And then he sticks out his jaw and says it again." The grin became a guffaw. "D'you see, Baron? He needed a hundred thou, not fifty."

Across the table, Alexander Baron took a swallow of his after-dinner Drambuie and smiled politely.

"And did you? Lend him the money, I mean."

J.T. was still chuckling. "Of course. How could I turn down such a creative request?"

"Indeed," Alex said pleasantly. "How could you?" His smile shifted to Whitney, sitting opposite him. "And you agree, Whitney?"

Whitney blinked. Dinner had seemed endless. She had only managed to get through it by keeping herself insulated from reality, as she'd learned to do years before when her father had begun to include her at his business dinners. By the time she'd left for the mainland a year later, she'd mastered the art of sensing when to smile or murmur a polite comment even though her thoughts were elsewhere.

Tonight had proven that her skills had not diminished. She'd gone through the meal saying little, raising her brows in a look of interest when it seemed appropriate, nodding her head now and then, although her father's occasional warning glance suggested he'd expected more from her.

But Alex seemed satisfied. At least, he'd left her alone—and that was the last thing she'd expected. She'd been knotted with tension all through the soup and salad, waiting for him to go on making those not so guarded innuendoes.

But he hadn't. He'd seemed content to ignore her throughout the meal, which was why it surprised her to look up now and find him watching her, the faintest curl of a smile on his lips.

There was something in the look that sent a whisper of anxiety dancing along her spine. Carefully, showing him nothing but a smile that was the civilized match of his, Whitney put down her coffee cup and then patted her mouth with a damask napkin.

"I'm sorry," she said, "I'm afraid I didn't catch that."

"Your father was just telling me a rather amusing anecdote about a business deal, one he hadn't had any intention of financing." Alex's smile twisted a little. "But when the plea for funds took an unexpectedly creative bent he found it impossible to refuse." He lifted his glass to his lips and took another swallow of the liqueur, although his eyes never left hers. "It's an interesting story, don't you think?"

He was baiting her into something, but what? "I suppose it is," she said carefully. "Actually, I don't pay much attention to——"

"What I mean is, the general public sees high finance as such cut and dried propositions. So much money lent out at so much interest for so many years—dull stuff, all of it." Alex leaned back in his chair and looked at her. "But there are times when the pot is sweetened in such imaginative ways."

"I'm sure it's quite interesting," Whitney said courteously. "But..."

The smile faded and his eyes, as cold as the sea after a storm, met hers.

"Interesting? Fascinating is more like it. No one would believe some of the things I've been offered when large sums are at stake."

A flush rose under Whitney's skin. His meaning was unmistakable. She glanced at her father, but J.T. was gazing into his liqueur as if he might read the future in the amber liquid. She drew a breath and then pushed back her chair. The scrape of it against the hardwood floor was shrill in the silence.

"I'm sure you could tell us tales that would make us gasp," she said calmly. "But I'm not much interested in business. So if you'll excuse me..."

That got her father's attention. He looked up and frowned. "Surely you're not going up so soon, Whitney."

"Yes, I am." Her voice was low-pitched but firm. "I'm sure you and your guest have important business to discuss."

J.T.'s eyes narrowed. "Whitney..."

"I'm tired, Father. It's been a long day."

Alex smiled. "And a longer evening," he said. "Isn't that right, Whitney?"

J.T. cleared his throat in warning. "My daughter traveled all day, just so she could be here tonight. Isn't that right, my dear?"

"How charming." Alex looked at her as if they shared some mutually amusing secret. "I'm flattered to hear it."

Angry words of denial rose in her throat, but she bit them back. He was waiting for her to rise to the bait again—she could see it in his eyes. But she wasn't going to give him the satisfaction.

Carefully, she dropped her napkin on the table. "Good night, gentlemen."

"To think she went to so much trouble, just for me."

J.T. cleared his throat again. "Perhaps you had better go up, my dear. It *is* getting late, and..."

Alex leaned back in his chair and folded his arms across his chest.

"Really, Turner, I'm touched."

Whitney spun toward him. "Don't be," she said, fairly spitting out the words. "My arrival had nothing whatsoever to do with you. In fact, if I'd known you were going to be here——"

J.T.'s face reddened. "Whitney!"

"For God's sake, Father, maybe you can sit there and take all this nonsense. But I——"

Alex put his hands flat on the table and leaned forward. "Interesting," he said softly. "Your memory's come back, despite your exhaustion."

The jibe caught her by surprise. "What?"

His smile was quick, almost feral. "Well, just before dinner, you seemed quite certain we'd never met before."

Whitney's teeth closed lightly on her bottom lip. "I didn't—I didn't say that."

"No?" His brows rose. "What did you say, then?"

"I said..." She hesitated. "I said I—I couldn't place you."

"And now you have. In fact, you've remembered enough about me to say that you'd never have come home if you'd known I was going to be here." The swift, chilling smile flashed across his face again. "Isn't it convenient for all of us that your memory lapse lasted long enough to get us through dinner?"

Whitney stared back at him. He was watching her with the same dispassionate interest with which a child might watch an ant scurry along the pavement before smashing it with his hand.

A shudder of distaste ran through her. That this man, who had so deceived her years ago, should now be seated across the table from her, was impossible. That he should be treating her and her father as if they were creatures trotted out for his amusement was incredible. And that her father should be behaving as if all that were perfectly acceptable was—God, it was intolerable!

She scraped back her chair and stood up. "I'm too tired to play games, Mr. Baron. If you'll excuse me..."

But he was as quick as she was. "I agree," he said, rising to his feet. "I've been on the go all day myself. Turner, if you've no objection, we'll postpone further discussion till tomorrow."

J.T. nodded. "No problem, Baron. Tomorrow's fine. How about breakfast? Say, at eight-thirty?"

Whitney felt the tension draining from her. It was almost over, then. She could, she told herself, manage to be gracious for the goodbyes.

Her lips stretched in what she hoped was a smile, and she turned to Alex.

"It's been—it's been interesting seeing you again, Mr...." His brows rose. "Alex," she said, correcting herself. As he came around the table, she forced herself to extend her hand. "I hope you have a safe journey."

His fingers closed around hers. "I haven't drunk enough this evening to make the staircase that perilous," he said dryly.

Whitney stared at him. "Are you—are you staying the night?"

Amusement glinted in his eyes. "Such a gracious hostess," he said softly. "I can see that the prospect of my staying in your home delights you."

Her chin lifted. "This is my father's home," she said quietly. "And he's free to do with it as he chooses."

"Whitney." J.T. cleared his throat. "I've put Alex in the gold room. Would you be good enough to show him to it?"

Let him find it himself, she wanted to say, just the way he found his way to this house the first time.

But there was a shadowed look in her father's eyes, almost a plea. It surprised her, so much so that she nodded. She had survived the worst of the evening; it would only take another few minutes to lead the way up the stairs, and then her duty would be discharged. She would never have to see Alexander Baron again.

She mounted the steps quickly and started down the hall. But Alex paused, and she had no choice but to do the same.

"This must be the Rogues' Gallery."

Whitney looked at him. It was how she had always referred to the dark oil portraits of Turner forebears that hung on the paneled walls. She was surprised that he remembered.

"Yes," she said.

He nodded. "A happy lot, aren't they? Are they all this dour?"

Whitney shrugged her shoulders. "I don't know," she said sullenly. "I've never noticed."

She had, of course. When she was a little girl, she'd spent hours gazing at these severe faces, wondering if any of her ancestors had ever known how to smile.

"Who's this gentleman?"

"My great-grandfather."

He moved slowly to the next painting. "And this?"

"My uncle."

"And this?"

Whitney puffed out her breath. "Look, if you want a tour of the place, I'm sure my father will be happy to arrange something tomorrow morning. But I'm tired. So if you don't mind..."

Alex made her a sweeping bow. "Forgive me, m'lady. Lead on."

The old, familiar taunt made her breath catch. She jerked around to face him, but his expression was blank.

"This way," she said, marching past him, head held high, never stopping until they reached the door at the end of the corridor.

"Your room," she said. "If you need anything, just ring for the housekeeper."

Alex caught her wrist as she turned away. "A good hostess would see to it that I have everything I want."

His voice was low; the lazy tone of amusement was back in it, and it brought a flush to Whitney's cheeks.

"If you need anything," she repeated, "I'm sure the housekeeper will be happy to oblige."

He laughed softly. "Thank you. But, having seen the lady, I think I'll pass."

She felt her flush deepening. "I meant towels," she said, forcing herself to meet his sardonic gaze. "Toothpaste. Or an extra pillow."

"Ah." He nodded, his expression one of complete innocence. "Yes, of course. I'll be sure to ring if I do." His hand tightened on her wrist. "Well, then, there's nothing left to do but say good night."

Something in his voice made her heart stumble. She had the sudden terrible desire to turn and run. Instead, she forced herself to speak calmly.

"Good night," she said.

But the pressure of Alex's hand held her fast.

"I hear you've done well in Los Angeles."

She nodded. "Yes."

He smiled. "Meals in a Minute, hmm? Not bad."

"Alex, look, I really am tired. So if you——"

"Are you happy?"

Her eyes met his. "Yes," she said quickly. "Of course I'm happy. My business is doing well, I've a handsome house in——"

"Ah, yes, I almost forgot." His smile grew crooked. "The Turners measure happiness differently from the rest of us. Houses, businesses, bank accounts..."

Whitney's eyes narrowed. "And how do you measure it, Alex? By the numbers of supplicants at your feet?"

He laughed. "Meaning you and your father."

"Meaning I've played your little game, and now I'd like to go to my room."

He stepped closer to her. "It's amazing, how little you've changed in all these years."

The unexpected softness in his voice startled her, and she looked up at him. His eyes were veiled by his lashes and his body was taut—she could read nothing in either his face or his stance—and yet she felt a sudden difference in him, as if he was waiting for something to happen.

For an instant, time spun backward. She thought of how many times they had stood like this in the past, bodies almost touching, breath intermingling, their voices pitched low so no one would hear them.

But what good were memories when they were all lies? Nothing that had happened between them had been real. Alex had played both her and her father for fools then, just as he was doing tonight.

"If you really think that," she said coolly, "you must have had more to drink than you should have."

He shook his head. "Some things don't change, Whitney."

"Everything changes." Her voice was sharp. "You know that better than anyone. Otherwise, you wouldn't be here tonight." Her eyes met his. "How does it feel to be calling the shots, Alex?"

His eyes darkened. "Suppose you tell me."

She tossed her head. "I can imagine! It must be wonderful to walk in here and know you're in command."

His smile was as cold as her voice. "And I can imagine how that makes you feel. The stable boy, come to visit with the rich folks. You must be thrilled."

Whitney drew in her breath. "There's no point to this conversation. If you don't mind——"

"You hated having me at the dinner table, didn't you?" His hand tightened on hers. "I could see it on your face—you looked as if each mouthful was enough to make you gag."

"That's enough. Look, you've made your point. You can buy and sell us now, so——"

"I used to wonder what this house was like. The furniture, the rooms... Even the Rogues' Gallery." He nodded his head toward the portraits on the wall. "Each time you talked about them, I tried to imagine how they looked."

"Well, now you've seen them. You can die happy."

He laughed softly. "I hate to disappoint you, baby, but I don't plan on dying any time soon. There's too much in life I haven't done yet."

"Starting with making J.T. Turner and his daughter crawl?"

"Ah, Whitney, Whitney. Our games used to be so much more subtle. Don't you think they were more fun that way?"

"Look, haven't you gotten what you wanted? My father capitulated..."

"But you haven't." He wasn't smiling any more; the look in his eyes was dark and chill. "You don't regret a damned thing, do you?"

It wasn't a question, but Alex expected an answer. She knew what he wanted—some conciliatory remark, some gesture that would make it clear she understood how their roles had changed since they'd last seen each other.

But she couldn't do it. And, even if she could, what was the purpose? Her father hadn't fooled anyone. Alex had known all along that the whole night had been a charade—J.T.'s hearty show of camaraderie, the elegant meal, her participation in it—it was all a bluff, and he was smart enough to have seen right through it.

They were caught in a web of lies, all of them. And she was tired of it.

Her eyes met Alex's. "You don't have any intention of lending my father the money he needs, do you?"

His brows rose. "Did I say that?"

"You don't have to. I know why you're here."

"Do you?"

Whitney tossed her head. "My father thinks it's because you see a good business deal..."

Alex laughed. "Oh, I do. Especially when it means acquiring the Turner assets. I mean, there's a special justice to that, after all."

Her eyes flashed as she remembered how he'd wrung twenty-five thousand dollars from her father nine long years ago.

"Considering how you got your start," she said coldly, "I'm sure there must be."

"Considering...?"

"Yes. Stepping up from the gutter into the company of the Turners must be quite an experience for you."

Alex's smile vanished. His eyes turned cold and flat. "Don't push me," he said softly.

The look and sound of him was frightening. But she had gone too far to stop; besides, her father had groveled enough for the both of them.

"You're wasting your time," she said, shaking free of his hand. "You were right about me, Alex. I haven't fallen at your feet. And I never will."

A sly smile curled across his mouth. "M'lady speaks. Perhaps someone should tell her that 'never' is a long, long time."

"You can laugh all you like. But I'm not going to grovel. You can bet on it."

Again, that sly smile twisted across his face. "Not even to save the old homestead?"

"The Turner Ranch? You wouldn't..." He laughed, and Whitney gritted her teeth together. "Damn you," she hissed. "You—you..."

"Now, now." His voice mocked her. "Daddy won't like it if you insult his guest."

"Exactly. *His* guest. Not mine. If it were up to me..."

He reached out lazily. Before she could move, his hand had curved around the nape of her neck.

"If it were up to you, I'd be sleeping out in the stables. Isn't that right, Whitney?"

"Yes." Her eyes flashed up at him. "That's where you belong. It's where you always belonged. I should never have——"

"No. You shouldn't have." His eyes grew dark, and he stepped closer to her. "But what the hell, the lady had a yen for something different, so she went slumming."

Her hand arced through the air, but he caught it before it connected with his cheek.

"Get out of this house," she whispered. Her voice shook. "Do you hear me? Get out!"

"Don't ask for something unless you're sure you want it." His voice was a whisper, like the hiss of a snake before it strikes. "You might regret it."

"When I tell my father——"

"Tell him what? That your pride means more to you than the Turner land? That you don't give a damn for what happens to it?" He laughed. "Well, then, don't let me stop you. Go on—run to Daddy. Tell him you want his only hope thrown out the door.''

Whitney stood staring at him. Alex Baron *was* their only hope, that was what her father had said. Without him, everything the Turners owned was lost.

Well, that didn't matter to her. It never had.

But it mattered to J.T. She thought again of how pale he'd looked earlier this evening. Was he ill, or was he only worried about the collapse of his empire? Suddenly, she knew it was impossible to separate one issue from the other. Her father and the world he'd created were the same: one could not survive without the other.

The burden that placed on her made her shoulders sag. Alex, reading her face, nodded.

"That's right," he said softly. "Think it over. Get your priorities straight. You were always good at that."

Whitney took a deep breath. "What is it you want from us?"

His teeth flashed in a quick smile. "Only what your father offered."

"I don't know what you think you're—I don't know what he said..."

His smile faded, and he reached out and touched his hand to her hair.

"Don't you?" She held her breath as he stepped close to her. "He said you'd be pleased to see me again. But the evening's almost over, and I'm still waiting to hear you tell me how happy you are."

Tears of frustrated rage rose in her eyes. "I hate you, do you know that?"

"Ah, such a sweet sentiment. And to think I had to wait all night to hear it."

"Why are you doing this? You've made your point. My father needs you..."

Alex's hand slipped from her nape to the back of her head. "But not you," he whispered. "Not you, Whitney."

"Is that what you want? To humiliate me more than you already have?"

He stared into her eyes, and then his gaze swept over her face, coming to rest finally on her mouth.

"I don't know what I want from you," he said, his voice thickening. "Damn you to hell, I don't..."

She cried out as he tilted her face up, but he caught the cry in his kiss. Nothing about it was erotic or even passionate; his mouth was hard, his teeth sharp. It was as if he was determined to show her his strength, to dominate her in a way he had not been able to do all evening.

Whitney moved against him, trying to pull free, and he turned and pushed her back against the wall. The weight of his body fell against hers.

"Don't," she said. "Don't——"

His tongue thrust into her mouth. The taste of him filled her, and suddenly a million memories flooded her mind, taking her back through a spiraling darkness to a place and time she had sworn to forget.

"Alex," she whispered, and the sound of his name was like a magic incantation. His kiss changed, the feel of his arms around her changed—the years slipped away as Alex gathered her in his arms.

His mouth gentled on hers, and she felt the harsh tension flow from his body, until only heat and desire were left.

She whimpered softly as his hands moved up her back, to her shoulders, to her throat. His hand spread into her hair, clasping her head and holding her still beneath his kiss.

Heat bloomed within her and flowed like liquid fire through her blood. It was as if the red-hot lava that flowed from Kilauea was swirling instead through her veins, melting her bones.

The world began to tilt. Andy, she thought...

She staggered when his hands closed on her shoulders and he thrust her from him. Her eyes opened blindly; it seemed to take forever until she could focus her gaze on his face.

"Andy," she whispered—and then she saw him, really saw him, and her blood, so heated only seconds before, became ice.

It was Alex who held her in his arms. His face was a mask, cold and deadly. His eyes were dark slits, his mouth a narrow slash. And his voice was as flat and alien as if he had fallen into this place from some strange planet.

"That's the way," he said, and he wiped the back of his hand across his mouth. "If you put your heart into it, I might just give Daddy that loan."

Bile rose in her throat. She turned and flew along the hall to her bedroom, her hand to her mouth. The door slammed shut behind her as she ran through the dark to the bathroom and leaned over the bowl.

A long while later, Whitney straightened up, then switched on the light. She peered into the mirror over the basin, wincing when the harsh fluorescent glare revealed her pale face and wide, startled eyes. Her glance fell to her mouth, still swollen from Alex's kiss. She put her hand to it, a hand that trembled as if she were running a fever.

Her eyes filled with tears. Nine years ago, Alex Baron had made a fool of her. He'd used her until she no longer served his purpose, and she'd hated him ever since.

But tonight he had taken her in his arms, and the world had become, for one miraculous moment, a place of joy and happiness.

How could that be? How?

Slowly, Whitney turned away and shut off the light. Darkness wrapped around her.

"Please," she whispered, to whatever ancient *tiki* might still be looking down on this island paradise. "Please help me."

But no answer came. All she could hear was the race of her own heart in the deep silence of the Polynesian night.

CHAPTER FIVE

WHITNEY was not used to sleeping late. As a child, she'd always been eager to start the day: the ranch's horses and colts were especially eager to greet someone with carrots in her pockets early in the morning.

In adulthood, sleeping in had become a luxury she couldn't afford. She had a daily catering business to run, which meant she had to be at the market at dawn to choose the freshest produce, the finest meats and fish.

That was why it was especially hard to feign sleep the next morning, when Pearl knocked lightly at her door. But she lay still, pretending she didn't hear the woman's quiet footfalls or the gentle clatter of silverware as her morning coffee was laid out on a table near the *lanai* door.

The last thing she wanted was to let anyone know she was awake. For all she knew, Pearl might be carrying a message from her father, asking Whitney to join Alex and him—and she had absolutely no intention of doing it.

She had done what she'd been brought here to do, she'd faced Alex Baron, and if she hadn't groveled at his feet she'd done the next best thing to it by making a fool of herself when he'd taken her in his arms and kissed her.

Not that it mattered. Alex had taken her by surprise and accomplished, in only a few moments, what he'd been trying to do the entire evening. He'd set out to humble her and he had. All she could hope now was that his revenge was sweet enough to give her father the loan he needed.

Whitney sighed as she tossed aside the blankets and rose from the bed. It was out of her hands anyway, she thought as she drew on her robe and padded across the room. This time tomorrow, she'd be heading back to L.A. and the life she'd created for herself there.

It was a good life, one that pleased her, and in some ways she owed it all to Alex. If he hadn't come along, she might have stayed on the ranch forever, torn between the need to be her own person and the duty to be J.T. Turner's daughter.

A bitter smile touched her lips as she poured her coffee. It was probably the only decent thing Alex Baron had ever done, and he didn't even know it.

She took her time showering and dressing, but the hands on the clock seemed immobile and she ended up pacing her room like a caged tiger. Wasn't the man ever going to leave? Finally, shortly after ten, a helicopter skimmed low over the house.

Goodbye, Alex, she thought, and she opened the door to her room and went down the stairs.

She was surprised to find her father still in the dining room, sitting at the table with the morning papers spread out before him and a cup of coffee in his hand. She'd half expected him to have flown off with Alex, to arrange for a transfer of funds—unless the loan hadn't gone through.

He looked up as she entered the room. "Whitney, my dear. Good morning. How did you sleep? Well, I hope."

She had hardly slept at all, but there seemed no point in saying so. Instead, she smiled politely as she went to the sideboard and poured herself a glass of fresh pineapple juice.

"Fine, thank you." She sat down across from him and opened her napkin. "How did your meeting go?"

Her father folded the paper and put it aside. "Very well," he said heartily. "Very well indeed."

Whitney let out a relieved breath. "Alex has agreed to the loan, then."

There was the briefest of pauses before J.T. responded. "We're close to an agreement," he said. "There are just a few details to be worked out."

"Good. I wondered if—I thought there might have been some difficulty."

J.T.'s bushy brows rose. "Why would you think that?"

"I don't know, I just did. I mean, dinner didn't go quite as smoothly as you'd hoped."

Her father added sugar to his cup, then stirred vigorously. "I thought it went rather well, all things considered. Baron didn't seem to mind the way you baited him. In fact——"

Whitney put down her glass of juice. "*I* baited *him*? Come on, Father. The man was laughing at us all night. As far as he's concerned, you and I are beneath contempt. Surely you know that."

"What I know," her father said smoothly, "is that we set out to win him over, and we did."

Whitney grimaced. "We set out to prostrate ourselves at his feet, you mean. All the rest of it—the talk about impressing him, about reminding him that we're Turners and he's not..."

J.T. shrugged his shoulders. "We made our point."

"Forgive me if I'm a little confused, Father, but you and I must have been at different tables last night."

"I agree, Baron was not quite as—well, as impressionable as I'd thought he might be. And he was a bit hard-edged. But I suppose it's understandable, from his vantage point. After all, he left here a common laborer, and now..."

"He left here a common thief." Whitney paused as the housekeeper entered the room with a fresh pot of coffee. After the door swung shut again, she leaned toward her father. "I just don't understand your attitude. Before he got here last night, you were singing a different tune. You were going to intimidate the hell out of Alexander Baron."

"Perhaps. But——"

"But he turned the tables on you. He made it clear that he holds all the cards." Her nostrils flared. "You might as well have served crow instead of beef at dinner, because crow is what we dined on."

J.T. put his hand to his forehead and massaged his temple. "I know this is difficult for you to accept, Whitney. But I've no choice. Turner Enterprises is in trouble, and..."

"...and the local banks wouldn't help." Her shoulders slumped in defeat. "I know. And I know you did what you had to do last night. It's just that it kills me that, of all the people in the world, Alexander Baron should be the one we have to turn to for help."

Her father nodded. "Don't you think I feel the same way? But I'm in a corner, Whitney. I have to take help where I can find it—and Baron's one of the few men with the money and the nerve to dabble in this kind of financial game."

"That only makes it harder to swallow. After all, he probably wouldn't be in that position if it weren't for you."

J.T. looked up. "What do you mean?"

"Well, just think about it. He probably made his first million out of the twenty-five thousand he extorted from you nine years ago."

Her father paled. "Whitney—for God's sake—you didn't say that to him?"

She shook her head. "No, I'm not that foolish. Heaven knows I wanted to, but I kept my mouth shut." She smiled grimly. "I doubt that reformed crooks like to be reminded of how they got their start in life."

Her father laughed shakily. "Exactly. We don't want to do anything to prejudice Baron's approval of that loan." His smile faded. "You will remember that, my dear—won't you?"

"There's nothing to worry about, Father. I won't be seeing Alex Baron again, remember?"

J.T. put his palms flat on the table and looked at her. "My back's against the wall, Whitney. Just keep that in mind. If Baron should turn me down..."

"Mr. Turner?" The housekeeper stood in the doorway. "There's a call for you, sir."

J.T. nodded. "I'll be right there." He pushed back his chair, got to his feet, and looked at Whitney. "We'll talk later. At dinner."

"Are you leaving, Father? I'd hoped we——"

"Or we'll talk tomorrow, just in case I'm delayed getting back." He gave her a quick smile. "How's that sound?"

Whitney stood up. "I won't be here then. Remember? I'm leaving in the..."

The door swung shut. Her father was gone; she was talking to an empty room.

Some things never changed. Maybe Alex was right.

The midday sun beat down on Hina Beach, turning the tiny grains of volcanic sand into a universe of dazzling black crystals. Except for the ceaseless beat of the sea against the shore, nothing stirred along the deserted crescent. There was not even a breeze to ruffle the dark green fronds of the coconut palms that backed against the cliff.

Clad in shorts and an oversize T-shirt, Whitney made her way down the narrow path that wound down to the beach. She hadn't come to Hina deliberately, she'd simply taken a Jeep from the ranch and set out with no specific destination in mind.

Half an hour later, when she found herself at the cliffs, she knew that wasn't true. Hina Beach had been her goal all along, even if she hadn't admitted it to herself.

If she were ever going to exorcise the ghosts that haunted her, there was no better place to start. Memories of Alex had kept her prisoner far too long.

The trail was overgrown and difficult. By the time she reached the thick shrubs that marked its last few yards, Whitney was breathing hard. She paused, took a final deep breath, then pushed her way through a tangle of undergrowth and stepped out on to the jutting rock that marked the trail's end.

A great feeling of peace swept over her. Yes, she thought, she had missed this place terribly. More than the ranch, more than the house she'd grown up in, Hina Beach was home.

A family of sandpipers, foraging for their dinner along the black sand, gave a flutter of alarm as Whitney jumped lightly to the ground. She stood motionless until the birds had accepted her, and then she turned in a slow circle and looked at this tranquil bit of paradise that was hers and hers alone.

It was as beautiful as she'd remembered. She felt her heart fill, felt a sudden tightness in her throat. So many memories. So many beautiful, bittersweet memories.

She shook herself. Enough, she thought. That wasn't why she'd come here. She set off briskly toward the sea. She had other remembrances of this place, ones that had nothing to do with Alex Baron. Her mouth firmed as she dropped her towel to the sand. Those were the ones she had to concentrate on, if this visit were to accomplish what it was meant to.

The surf broke like lace across her toes, and she lifted her face to the sun, closed her eyes, and let her senses take over. She savored the heat of the summer afternoon, breathed in the rich scent of the Pacific, felt the power in the beat of the waves against the shore.

Nalani, her old nurse, had loved to spin stories of the Old Ones.

"Be like them, child," she used to say. "Be one with Nature."

Nalani's gentle counsel seemed to echo in her head. She inhaled deeply, let her breath out, then inhaled again. Slowly, the tension began to flow from her body.

When she finally opened her eyes, she felt at peace. Coming here had been the right thing to do.

She turned and trotted back up the beach, peeled off her shorts and T-shirt, and dropped them to the sand. She was wearing a bikini underneath, an old one she'd dredged from the bottom dresser drawer. Nine years ago, it had been little more than three scraps of emerald green silk. Now it barely covered her.

She hesitated, then reached back, unhooked her top, and tossed it aside. She'd often swum and sunbathed here without wearing anything at all. Not the times when Alex had been with her, of course. She'd even kept her T-shirt on then. The thought of letting him see her in her bikini had scared her as much as it had excited her.

But that hadn't kept him from touching her. Whitney's breath caught as she remembered the heat of his hand against her flesh as he'd slid it up under her T-shirt, the shock of his fingers cupping her flesh, the little whimpering sound she'd made when he'd unclasped her bikini bra and her breasts had tumbled free into his waiting palms...

A shudder raced through her. No. She didn't want to think about that. She didn't want to think about anything. All she wanted to do was close her eyes and give herself up to the silence.

She sank to the towel. After a moment, her lashes fell to her cheeks, and she slept.

Whitney awoke with a start, heart racing, unsure for the moment of where she was, still caught in some dark, unhappy dream that had involved a shadowy figure, a man, one whose face she could not see.

The sun was directly overhead and beating down with a ferocity she'd almost forgotten. She sat up slowly and put her hands to her face. She was hot—too hot. Her skin felt parched.

She rose and walked slowly to the water's edge. A wave rolled in and the dying edge of it broke across her toes. Shivering, she danced back a step before the next wave could reach her. It was the contrast between her over-heated skin and the sea that made it feel so chill.

Well, there was only one thing to do about that. She took a deep breath.

"Okay," she whispered, and then she let out a wild shriek. "Ready or not," she yelled, just as if she were still twelve years old, and she raced headlong into the surf.

The shock took her breath away. She yelped, and then she took a mouthful of air and dived under the curl of a wave. She came up past the breakers, gasping and laughing, then rolled onto her back and let herself drift. She could feel the water for what it was, now—a warm, silken bath.

Alex had loved the feel of it. They'd played in the sea for a long time, splashing and laughing like kids, until his hand had accidentally brushed her flesh and then—and then . . .

"Stop it," she said fiercely.

She was here to get rid of her ghosts, not to resurrect them. But the exhilaration that had gripped her moments ago had slipped away. She sighed, then rolled over and struck out for shore.

The breaking waves carried her to the shallows. She stood slowly, letting the water stream like gossamer from her body, and then she began walking out of the sea.

The sun was in her eyes, blinding her, and she closed her eyes against it while she walked. Her breasts rose as she raised her arms and combed her soaked hair back from her face with her fingers.

Ankle-deep in the warm sea, she paused. Goose bumps rose on her skin. She felt something, sensed something different. No. Not something. Someone.

A shadow—a figure—loomed before her, blocking out the sun.

It was Alex.

Whitney froze, arms upraised. Alex, she thought crazily, Alex was here, appearing from out of nowhere just as he had so many years ago, dressed in cut-off denims and nothing else, like an apparition conjured up out of dust motes whirling in the sunlight.

He took a step forward. "Hello, Whitney." His voice was soft, but there was an almost palpable tension about him.

Cover yourself, her brain shrieked. But she felt paralyzed, too stunned to move or to speak.

A faint smile tilted across his mouth. "You look like the goddess Hina, just emerging from the sea."

Still, she said nothing. His gaze swept across her face, lingering briefly on her parted lips before slipping like a lover's caress to her naked breasts.

It was as if he had touched her. Whitney felt her breasts rise, felt her nipples tighten. Alex's eyes met hers, and the sudden flare of heat in their pale green depths seemed to leap the distance between them and curl like wildfire through her loins.

Her heart thudded. If she went to him now, he would take her here, on this wild crescent of sand, with only the sea and the sun to bear witness. She had only to walk to him, to move into his arms...

The madness of the thought was enough to set her free. Slowly, her arms fell to her sides. Her eyes moved past him, to where her towel lay in the sand, and she began walking toward it, fighting the instinct to cover her breasts with her hands.

Alex was the intruder here, not she. A tight knot of anger coiled low in her belly, and she passed him without comment or acknowledgment, her head held high.

When she reached her towel, she picked it up and wrapped herself in it. Then she took a deep breath, and turned to face him.

"What are you doing here, Alex?"

He chose not to answer the question. "You told me about Hina the first time you brought me here, do you remember?"

Of course she remembered. She had told him the legend of the Polynesian maiden who'd been separated from her lover by the jealous gods.

Nothing will ever separate us, Whitney, he'd said. *Liar. Liar.*

Her shoulders lifted in a careless shrug. "Did I? I'm sorry, Alex, but I really don't recall. There are so many Hawaiian legends."

"You said she risked death, leaving the sea, to find her lover. You said——"

"I'm sure you could tell me the entire story, Alex. What I'd rather have you tell me is the reason you were spying on me."

He laughed softly, scuffing his bare toes in the sand as he walked toward her.

"Sorry about that. It occurred to me when I was halfway down the cliff that you'd probably be surprised to see me."

Whitney's brows lifted. "Surprised is an understatement. You still haven't explained what you're doing here."

"I came looking for you," he said. "Your father didn't know where you'd gone, so——"

"My father knows you're here?"

"Yes. Of course. Didn't he tell you I'd be back?"

Whitney stared at him. "No," she said flatly. "He did not."

Alex bent and picked up a handful of sand. "I told him what I'd decided to do," he said. The sand trickled through his fingers and drifted away. "He seemed satisfied. I'd have thought he'd have mentioned it to you."

"He only said you and he were close to an agreement about the loan."

"And that pleased you."

Whitney looked at him. "Of course."

"Yeah. I thought it would." A cool smile tilted at the corners of his mouth. "Hell, you wouldn't want all last night's efforts to have been for nothing."

Color rose in her cheeks. "I'm afraid I don't see what any of this has to do with me, Alex. If you and my father have an agreement to hammer out——"

"We've already done that. I'll lend Turner Enterprises the money it needs—once I'm satisfied it's a worthwhile investment."

"I'm sure your accountants will say it is," she said briskly. "Now, if you don't mind——"

"My accountants haven't a damn thing to do with it."

"Your auditors, then. Whomever."

Alex shook his head. "It's my decision, Whitney. Nobody else's."

Why was he looking at her that way? She felt as if he were measuring her, as if he were waiting for something to happen. Whitney began to feel uneasy.

"I'm not really interested in the details, Alex, although I'm sure my father will be. Now, I'd like to get dressed. So if you'd please leave..."

His eyes narrowed. "I really think you *should* be interested in the details, Whitney."

"I can't imagine why, especially since you and I have nothing to say to each other."

A slow, tight smile curved across his mouth. "Haven't we?"

Whitney's eyes flashed with anger. "Look, I don't know what your problem is. But I'm not going to stand here and let you——"

"I've got to hand it to you, baby. Here you are, naked as a jaybird, and you're still determined to play lady of the manor."

His voice was cold, and there was an element of malice in his words that frightened her. But she wasn't going to let him know that, not if it took all the courage she had to face him down.

"I am not naked," she said quietly. "And I wouldn't be standing here at all, if you were any kind of gentleman. If we must have this conversation, surely we could have it an hour from now, in the library."

Alex's teeth glinted in his tanned face. "That's right. I'm not a gentleman, and don't you forget it."

"How could I possibly? You take every opportunity to remind me."

"Just as you take every chance you can to remind me that you're a Turner."

She drew a deep breath. "Let's get something straight," she said softly. "I did not invite you here, Alex. Not to this beach. Not to this ranch. And certainly not to dinner last night. So if you don't like the way things are going——"

He laughed. "And a lovely dinner it was." He took a step toward her. "Did you and Daddy wager on whether I'd try to slurp the soup out of the bowl?"

"This is ridiculous. I'm not going to stand here and——"

He reached out and caught her by the shoulder as she started past him.

"But it didn't go the way you and J.T. expected, did it?" A chill smile tilted at his mouth. "Hell, I was half tempted to pick up the soup bowl just to see what you and J.T. would do. You were so desperate to keep me happy, you'd probably have followed suit."

Whitney twisted out from under his grasp. "You're wrong," she said coldly. "I'd have told you that you were a pig. And, if it had been up to me——"

"But it isn't." There was a silence, and then Alex turned away. "You're right, of course. You didn't ask me here." She watched as he tucked his hands into his back pockets and stood looking out to sea. "Your father did."

She waited for him to say something more. After a few seconds, she cleared her throat.

"And will you help him?"

A muscle knotted in his jaw. "I don't know."

"You don't—what do you mean, you don't know?"

Alex swung toward her. "What do you know of your father's situation?"

Whitney shrugged her shoulders. "Not much. I know he's in debt, that there's some kind of cash-flow problem..."

"A cash-flow problem?" His lips drew back from his teeth. "That's putting it mildly. It's more like a no-flow problem. Turner Enterprises is verging on collapse."

"Surely that's a bit melodramatic. My father needs a loan, yes. But——"

"He's losing money, thousands a day."

She stared at him. "I don't understand."

Alex shrugged. "That's the trouble. Nobody understands—except, maybe, the people who work for your father."

Whitney swallowed dryly. "But—you're going to help him."

"Maybe."

"What do you mean, maybe? You said——"

"I said he needs help. But I'm not a philanthropist. I'll lend your father what he needs—once I'm convinced there's something in it for me."

She looked at him, puzzled. "And how will you decide? A little while ago, you said your decision didn't depend on anybody but yourself. No accountants, no auditors..."

Alex nodded, his eyes on hers. "They've already done their jobs, Whitney. I've read their reports."

"And?"

"And now, I do mine." He put his hands on his hips; an impersonal smile played across his lips. "It's an unorthodox method. I think the *Wall Street Journal* described it as a Baron Barometer." The smile broadened. "But it's worked for me so far."

Whitney puffed out her breath. "Look, I'm sure my father will find all this fascinating. Why don't we go back to the house and——"

"What I do when I'm about to bail a company out," he said, his voice cutting across hers, "is roll up my sleeves, leave my briefcase in my car, and get down into the trenches with the troops."

"Well, that's colorful. What's it mean in English?"

Alex shrugged. "It means I do some low-key poking around. I talk to people, ask questions, take a firsthand look at things for myself. I immerse myself in the business before tossing it a lifeline."

"Meaning, you want to make sure the lifeline's not going to turn into an anchor and drag you under."

He looked at her in surprise. "Yeah. Exactly."

She shrugged her shoulders. "It's kind of like what I did before I opened Meals in a Minute. The idea sounded good—on paper. But I didn't want to commit myself until I'd scouted around."

"So you checked things out, talked with people..."

"Yes. I was lucky enough to have a friend who knew her way around Los Angeles—I mean, I was a newcomer, after all. And it helped enormously that she was a chef—she knew lots of caterers, they trusted her—she got more information in a month than I could have gotten in..." Her words faded away, and she stared at Alex. "What's that look for?"

"I was just thinking how handy it was that our methods are so similar." He bent and retrieved the top to her bikini, then held it out to her on one finger. "Would you like to put this scrap on, or shall I carry it for you?"

Whitney flushed and decided it was wisest to ignore the question.

"What do you mean, it's handy our methods are similar?"

Alex grinned as he tucked the bit of green silk into his back pocket. "It means," he said, taking her elbow as they began strolling toward the cliff, "that you'll approve of my plan."

Whitney gave him a quick glance. There was a quality to his voice that worried her, a sureness, an almost silken certainty. But about what?

"What plan?"

"Well, you've already outlined the basics. If I'm going to assess Turner Enterprises accurately, I'll need to work with someone who knows J.T. Turner intimately.'' They reached her discarded T-shirt and shorts, and he bent and scooped them up. ''And someone who knows the islands and the customs.''

Whitney nodded. ''Yes, that makes sense.''

Alex tossed her the shirt; she gave him a steady look and, after a moment, he turned his back.

''Above all, this person must be someone your father's people will trust. Someone they'll see as his surrogate.''

''A second-in-command, you mean?'' Whitney's voice was muffled as she drew the T-shirt over her head. No bra, she thought immediately, but short of asking Alex to give her the bikini top—which would only have made matters worse—there was nothing she could do about it. The shirt was loose enough, she thought, as she tugged it over her breasts. ''But my father's never had a second-in-command.''

''No. But he has a surrogate.''

''A surrogate? J.T.?''

Alex glanced over his shoulder, then swung toward her. ''Yes.'' A sly smile edged across his face, and Whitney took a quick step back.

''You can't mean me!'' He said nothing, and she swallowed hard. ''That's crazy. I don't know anything about Turner Enterprises.''

Alex shrugged. ''I don't expect you to. But you carry the Turner name. You'll have access to people and places that would be closed to me.''

''I've been away for nine years. The islands have changed.''

''The people haven't. You were born here. You know how things are done.''

''No. I can't.''

His eyes narrowed. ''Can't—or won't?''

''I have a business to run on the mainland. I can't just——''

Alex smiled. "Sally Copeland is a very capable lady, so I hear."

"My assistant? How do you know that?"

He laughed. "I told you, I've done my homework. All I need now is your cooperation." His smile faded. "You do want me to lend J.T. the money he needs, don't you?"

Whitney shook her head. "Are you saying—are you telling me you won't help him unless I agree to this?"

Alex's mouth narrowed. "I've defined the terms of the agreement, Whitney. The rest is up to you."

She watched, stunned, as he turned and strode toward the base of the cliff. The muscles in his shoulders knotted as he grasped the overhanging rock and hoisted himself up, and then he turned and looked back at her.

"Well?" he said. He held out his hand. "Are you with me, Whitney?"

She kept staring at him, waiting for him to smile, to laugh, to somehow let her know this had all been nothing but a bad joke. But his face was stern, his expression unforgiving.

Finally, when it was clear there was no other alternative, Whitney walked toward him.

"Not through choice," she said.

Alex's face darkened. "No." His voice was flat and soft, so soft she had to strain to hear it. "Never that."

He turned and started up the trail. By the time she'd scrambled up the rock, he'd vanished from view.

CHAPTER SIX

THE Jeep bearing the Turner Ranch logo bounced along the potholed road that snaked south from Hawi, a rooster tail of brown dust trailing in its wake. Cattle grazed beside the road, belly deep in the rich grass of the Kohala Mountains, as unconcerned by the noisy passage of the Jeep as they were by the *paniolo* riding herd among them on horseback.

Alex shifted down gear as the road climbed a steep ridge, then glanced over at Whitney.

"What's our next stop?" he said, raising his voice so she could hear him over the whine of the engine.

She looked down at the notebook in her lap. "Your choice," she said. "We can head east to the Hamakua coast—J.T. has some cane fields near Hilo. Or we can go down to Kona. There are three—no, four—Turner coffee farms near Captain Cook."

"Off Napoopoo Road. Yeah, I checked the report this morning." Alex nodded thoughtfully. "Okay. Next stop, the west coast."

Whitney clutched at the dashboard as the Jeep hit a rut. "If we make it to the highway in one piece," she said.

Alex gave her a quick smile. "Sorry. I guess I should have listened to Jim Sachs and taken the main road."

"No, you were right. We'd never have gotten a good look at what's been done with these cattle if we had. So, what do you think? Would these experimental breeds work for the ranch?"

He sighed. "Well, I'm not an expert on livestock. But from what we heard and saw this morning—yes, I think so. Sachs was pretty convincing. Read me the notes you have on him again."

"Let's see..." Whitney opened her notebook and thumbed through the pages. "Here we are. Sachs worked for J.T. for almost five years until the Parker people hired him away. Kichiro said he was the best manager the ranch had had in years."

"He did, huh? I suspected as much. But the old man was absolutely closemouthed when I questioned him."

Whitney smiled. "He's like that with everybody."

"Go on. What else did he say?"

She glanced down at her notes. "He told me that Sachs wanted to implement some new techniques to improve the stock—he wanted to enhance bloodlines by breeding some of the cows to King Ranch bulls..."

"Isn't the King Ranch in Texas?"

She nodded. "Yes. Sachs wanted to buy some frozen sperm and have it flown in."

Alex grinned wickedly. "Technology can take all the pleasure out of life, can't it?"

"He wanted to make some fairly drastic feed changes, too," Whitney said, ignoring the jibe although a faint wash of pink rose in her cheeks. "And when he couldn't push any of his ideas through, he quit in frustration."

"And went to work for the opposition."

She nodded. A few days ago, she'd have smiled at hearing Hawaii's world-famous Parker Ranch described as the 'opposition.' At two hundred and fifty thousand acres, it dwarfed the Turner spread and all others on the Big Island. But the techniques that had been successful for the Parkers would work just as well for the Turner operation. It was just that no one had been able to get them approved.

"Exactly." She closed the notebook and shifted in her seat until she was facing Alex. "We keep running into the same problem. J.T.'s insistence on running everything has led to a situation where nobody does anything."

Alex sighed. "That's the way it looks, all right. Your father doesn't like to delegate authority. I suppose it worked when he could shuttle from operation to operation. But he's involved himself in too many things over the last few years—hotel development on Oahu, condos on Maui..."

"And now he's spread too thin."

"Right. So, when a decision needs to be made, no one wants to make it because they're going to be second-guessed by J.T. Add on to that the financial setbacks he's suffered..."

"The stock market turnaround..."

"Uh-huh. J.T.'s house of cards came tumbling down." Alex slowed the Jeep as they went around a narrow curve in the road. "Well, at least we've begun to get some answers—thanks to you."

It was amazing, how much pleasure the simple words gave her. "I appreciate the compliment. But you're the one who asked the right questions, Alex."

"I could have asked questions from now until next year. Island people are amazingly closemouthed. Like Kichiro, they've no wish to talk to outsiders. But they're glad to help Miss Whitney any way they can."

She smiled. "I can't get over how many of them remember me," she said softly. "Sometimes I almost feel as if I'd never left the islands."

"Why did you leave?"

The gruff suddenness of the question caught her by surprise. She and Alex had been working side by side for a week now, and their relationship had gone from polite restraint to grudging respect to something she'd never expected—an easy compatibility that made her look forward to each day. But they had avoided anything that might even seem personal; their conversation dealt with the Turner businesses, with occasional forays into bits and pieces of Hawaiian folklore and geography.

Now, with one simple question, Alex had brought home just how fragile their new relationship really was. Whitney felt the smile fade on her lips, felt the old familiar tightness lodge just beneath her heart.

Because of you, she thought, because you made it impossible for me to live in a place where love had died.

"I'd have thought you had everything you wanted here," he said. "The right connections. Money. Power..."

Yes. Those were the things he'd always wanted; why would he think anyone would want anything else?

"How simple you make it sound," she said quietly.

He looked at her, then at the road. "It is simple." His voice had gone cold and flat. "Anyone who thinks differently is a damned fool."

At least he was honest about it. But he could afford to be honest now; those were the things that mattered to him. He had accumulated them all. Nine years ago, he hadn't had anything—except for a girl who would have given her life for him, a girl who'd loved him more than life itself.

A lump rose in Whitney's throat, and she swallowed past it. Say something he'll understand, she told herself.

"Maybe I—maybe I just wanted the chance to prove myself."

A quick smile flashed across his face. "There's a remark I just love," he said with cool sarcasm. "Funny, but the only people I've ever heard it from are the ones who were born with silver spoons in their mouths."

"What's that supposed to mean?"

Alex shrugged his shoulders. "It's the 'poor little rich girl' syndrome. San Francisco's full of women who run around trying to 'prove' themselves." He shook his head. "They've grown up in the lap of luxury, gone to the best schools—and now they're out there, working nine to five, playing at being secretaries and executives."

Whitney lifted her chin. "Well, I'm really sorry to disappoint you, Alex. But I'm not one of them. I work damned hard at my job. If you'd checked my company out half as well as you claimed, you'd know that."

He glanced at her, then looked back at the road. "You're right," he said grudgingly. "You do. My apologies." He lifted one hand from the wheel and flexed his fingers. "I guess I'm tired—I don't usually get carried away with generalities."

"And, before you ask, I built Meals in a Minute without any help from my father. I worked as a caterer's assistant and banquet manager for almost two years, saving every dollar I could until——"

Alex sighed. "Look, I said I was sorry." They had reached the intersection with the main road. He braked, checked for traffic, then swung out on to the tarmac. "So, how did you do it?"

"How did I do what?"

"Make a go of Meals in a Minute."

She relaxed. "Didn't your investigators find that out?"

Alex grinned. "My people are good. I can tell you the names of your accounts, how long each has been with you, even what they ordered last. I can tell you your net worth..."

She looked at him in surprise. "You checked on all that? But what has it to do with lending my father the money he needs?"

"Nothing. I was curious about you, that's all."

"Why?"

"Why not? It's not every day a girl leaves everything behind and sets out on her own. I wanted to know what kind of woman you'd grown into." He glanced at her.

"My people tell me you've done well. They say you ran in the black almost from the start. That's a remarkable feat for a new company."

It was impossible not to preen a little. She was proud of her success, prouder still that she owed it to no one but herself.

"Yes," she said agreeably, "it is."

Alex laughed. "Well, how did you pull it off?"

She smiled to herself. "Oh, the usual," she said smugly. "Careful planning. That sort of thing."

"Discounted purchases? Tight control of advertising dollars?"

Laughter bubbled from her throat. "If you really want to know, it was a little more basic than that. I'd go out and sign up a client, then race back to my apartment and cook her a week's worth of meals—assuming her deposit cheque cleared quickly enough for me to buy the foods I needed. If it didn't, I'd invent excuses to explain why I had to push the delivery date back."

Alex glanced at her. "Ah, yes. What might be called judicious inventory control."

She nodded. "I usually describe it as hands-on management, but I like your description better. It sounds much more professional."

He glanced into the mirror, then stepped on the gas and moved into the passing lane.

"You're talking to an expert at coining phrases." He grinned. "When I was seventeen and still wet behind the ears, I talked my way into a job as an assistant cook on a freighter from San Francisco to Yokohama. The captain wanted somebody with experience and I said yeah, that was me, all right, that I'd worked as a steward's assistant on a yacht for a year."

"A steward's assistant? What's that?"

He laughed. "Damned if I know. But he bought the story."

Whitney smiled. "What happened when he realized you had no experience? Was he angry?"

Alex shook his head. "Oh, I had the experience. I just hadn't gotten it aboard a ship."

"I don't follow you."

"Well, I figured all an assistant cook had to do was dish out food and clean up the galley, and hell, I'd been peeling potatoes and slopping out chow at the Boys' Home all my life."

She looked at him. "An orphanage?"

"Yeah. That's where I grew up. Everybody had assigned chores—and mine were in the kitchen. It wasn't the worst job—at least it meant you could cadge an extra serving of meat loaf once in a while." He shuddered. "But I can't look at a pan of dishwater to this day without turning green."

Whitney smiled. "From assistant cook to CEO. That must have been an interesting journey."

"It was. Sometimes I still can't believe I made it. I remember how scared I was when I set up my first corporation; I ran it out of my apartment, the same as you. But I made it sound as if I had a big office, with lots of employees. 'Baron Investments,' I'd say when I answered the phone, 'one moment please,' and then I'd drop my voice half an octave and pretend I'd just picked up the line." He sighed. "It's amazing how creative you can be when you have hardly any capital."

Whitney's smile faded. Hardly any capital? Was that what he called the twenty-five thousand dollars he'd extorted from her father? "But I'm sure you managed."

Her voice was cool, a little remote, but Alex didn't seem to notice. He looked at her and smiled boyishly, almost proudly.

"Yup. Not that it was easy. Those first months, getting started, never knowing if I was going to make it from day to day..."

Whitney stared at him. So, she thought, this was the success story he'd concocted. Poor boy makes good. Everybody liked that kind of thing.

It was a damned lie. And it was too bad she couldn't tell him that she knew the truth. Did he think J.T. hadn't told her? Or was he just so used to telling his lie that he'd begun to believe it himself?

Alex was still talking, going on and on about the start of Baron Investments with almost boyish eagerness. It was a story that probably knocked them dead back in San Francisco, but to someone who knew the truth, it was—it was appalling. The audacity of the man was overwhelming.

"I'm sure it's a fascinating story, Alex. But I'm tired. If you don't mind, I'm going to try and get some rest. Wake me when we reach Kona."

She put her head back and closed her eyes. She could sense his displeasure, feel his anger. When he finally spoke, it was almost a relief.

"What's the matter, Whitney? Was I boring you?"

She shrugged her shoulders. "I told you, I'm sure your story's interesting. But..."

"But not to a Turner." His hands flexed on the steering wheel. "That's the bottom line, isn't it?"

She swiveled toward him, eyes flashing, caution—for the moment, anyway—forgotten.

"That's right," she said softly. "Especially not to a Turner. So you might as well save your breath."

His mouth twisted. "You never give an inch, do you?"

She stared at him and then she looked away. "No. Not to you."

The brakes squealed as he pulled the wheel hard to the right. The Jeep jounced onto the shoulder of the road, then came to a wrenching stop.

Alex swung toward her, his eyes blazing with dark fury.

"Okay," he said, "okay, I've had it. For a while there, I thought we'd made some progress. I mean, we've gotten through the past few days without taking potshots at each other."

His anger was like a dark presence. It frightened her, and she clasped her hands together so he wouldn't see them shake.

"Yes," she said carefully. "I was thinking the same thing. I guess it only shows how wrong we both were."

He glowered at her, and then he slammed his fist against the steering wheel.

"Goddammit, what more do you want? I'm willing to bury the past."

"You? You're willing?" She stared at him incredulously. "Am I supposed to thank you for that?"

"No." His voice was gruff. "Hell, I know better than to ever expect thanks from a Turner."

"That's good. Because——"

"But I'm not going to crawl. So if that's what you're waiting for..."

What had she been waiting for? He was right: she'd been waiting for something the last week, but what?

Not that it mattered now. The fragile truce they'd constructed had fallen apart. She should have known it would.

She turned away from him and stared blindly out the window. "I don't want you to crawl," she said in a tight voice.

"Then why are you acting this way? We meant something to each other once..."

"Did we? I've forgotten."

He said something sharp and ugly, and then his hand closed hard on her shoulder and he forced her back against the door.

"You're a coldhearted bitch, do you know that?"

Whitney felt a little whisper of fear move along her skin. "You'd better let go of me, Alex. I'm not going to put up with this kind of treatment from you."

His mouth twisted. "Spoken like a true lady of the manor." He leaned closer to her. "But you'll take whatever I dish out, baby. And we both know it." A sly grin etched itself across his face. "What would you tell Daddy if his loan didn't come through?"

She stared at him. "What's that supposed to mean?"

"You're a smart lady. Figure it out for yourself."

"But you promised my father you'd lend him the money."

His teeth glinted in a quick smile. "Correction. I promised him I'd consider it."

"Come on, Alex, don't play games. You said this trip would give you the information you needed to make a decision."

He nodded. "Yeah, that's what I said, all right."

"That's why I came along. You said you needed me to—to help you."

"And you have." His voice was soft, almost a caress. She drew back as he leaned toward her. His hand brushed lightly across her breasts as he unhooked her seat belt. "You've been an enormous help. Didn't I just tell you that a little while ago?" She held her breath as he trailed his index finger down the side of her face, then across her mouth. "In fact, we work well as a team—you've got to admit that."

There was something in his eyes that frightened her. He was calm—very calm, the way the sea could be before a storm. Standing on the cliffs above Hina Beach, Whitney had once seen a *tsunami* building far out on the Pacific. The giant wave had reared into the sky with almost supernatural power, but what had been most terrifying was the way the ocean before it lay flat and smooth, as if it were waiting, waiting...

She forced herself to stay calm. "Get to the point, Alex. What is it you want from me?"

There was a silence, and then he nodded his head. "That's a good question," he said softly. "You asked it the other night, remember? I had no answer—then."

"But you have one now."

He nodded again. "Yes." His eyes followed the slow drift of his finger across her lips, and then he raised his eyes to hers. "At first, I thought I wanted you in my bed."

The bluntness of his answer brought bright patches of crimson color to her cheeks.

She slapped his hand away. "It'll be a cold day in hell before that happens," she said sharply.

Alex's brows rose. "Don't be so quick to say things you're liable to regret."

Whitney stared at him. "Not even you could be that despicable," she whispered.

He grinned. "Flattery will get you nowhere. I'm not the gallant sort, remember? Where I come from, chivalry is for suckers."

"If you really think I'd sleep with you just to—if you think my father would even permit such a thing..."

Alex laughed softly. "I didn't plan on asking his permission, Whitney."

"If he even thought—if he had any idea..."

His hand slipped to the nape of her neck. "You're on the wrong track, sweetheart." He shifted his weight, and suddenly they were only a breath apart. "This hasn't a damned thing to do with J.T. Turner, or the loan he wants. This is between you and me, Whitney. It's an old score—and it's past time we settled it."

He moved quickly, pinning her back against the seat before she could stop him.

"No," she said, twisting against him.

But his mouth was already on hers. His kiss was harsh, almost cold, and she endured it in silence.

Alex drew back and looked into her face. "Kiss me back, damn you."

"I hate you," she whispered.

He caught her by the shoulders and shook her. "Did you hear me? I said kiss me."

"No." Her eyes filled with tears. "No, I won't. There's a limit to what you can demand of someone."

His face twisted. "I remember a time when you wanted to be in my arms," he said. "I remember a time when the taste of you was as sweet as passionfruit."

"Don't," she whispered. "I beg you—don't."

Alex cupped her face in his hands. "Tell me you remember, too," he said softly.

"No." Whitney shook her head in denial. "I don't."

He bent to her and kissed her, his mouth gentle as it captured hers.

"Your eyes are like sapphires," he whispered, and suddenly the years fell away, and she was lost.

"Alex," she sighed, and her mouth opened to his.

He groaned as she put her hands against his chest. "Yes," he murmured, "yes, that's the way. Let me taste you. Let me..."

She whimpered softly as his hand moved over her, tracing the length of her neck, the shape of her shoulder, the taut outline of her breast.

"Tell me you want me," he said. "Let me hear you say it."

"Alex..."

His fingers moved lightly across her breast, across the tightly budded nipple, and she moaned and lifted her arms to him, winding them tightly around his neck.

"Tell me you want me as I want you." He took her hand from his neck and brought it down between them so that she could feel the power of his aroused body.

"That's what you do to me," he said in a ragged whisper. "It's what you've always done to me."

"No." She closed her eyes and shook her head in denial. "No."

He brought her hand to his mouth and kissed the palm, then placed it against his cheek.

"Yes," he said, and then he drew her into his arms and kissed her again. A lifetime seemed to pass before he finally raised his head and held her gently from him.

"Look at me," he whispered.

Her eyes opened slowly and focused on his face, taut and drawn with desire.

"I've been to bed with a lot of women in the past nine years, Whitney." She cringed and turned away, but he clasped her chin and forced her face to his. "Let me finish," he said roughly. His eyes swept over her, and he let out his breath. "A lot of women. But never one that made me forget how badly I wanted you."

"Am I supposed to feel flattered?"

He laughed softly, and his thumb moved lightly across her bottom lip.

"Don't tell me you haven't thought about how it would have been between us."

Her head was swimming. Of course she had thought about it, night after night, year after year. But she couldn't tell him that.

"No," she said. "I never did." The lie was bitter on her tongue. But it was what he deserved. Why was he doing this? Why?

His eyes darkened. "I don't believe you."

"I don't care what you believe. I've been busy. My business..."

"Have there been men?"

"Didn't your investigators tell you?" she said, stalling for time.

His mouth twisted. "I want to hear it from you."

She knew what he was asking: not if she had been with anyone, but if anyone had made her senses soar as he had, nine long years before.

No one had. Only in Alex's arms had she felt that hot, sweeping flush of desire, that sweet willingness to be both conquered and conqueror.

His hand tightened on her jaw, and she looked up. His eyes were on hers, his gaze fierce and proprietorial.

"Answer me," he demanded. "Have there been others?"

A wave of panic washed over her. God, what power he would have if he knew the truth!

"Yes." She spoke the lie calmly. "Of course there have. Did you think you'd spoiled me for anyone else?"

He smiled, and the coldness of it made her breath catch.

"No," he said. "Not when I didn't have the chance to finish what I'd only begun." His hand skimmed over her throat, then closed lightly around it. "But I'm going to, my sweet. I'm going to see to it that you can never look at a man again without thinking of me."

Her heart seemed to skip a beat. "Stop trying to frighten me, Alex. I don't for a minute believe that forcing a woman is your style."

He laughed. "Who said anything about force?" he whispered, and his hand slipped to the back of her head, his fingers tangling in the pale spill of her hair as he tilted her face to his. "What I had in mind was something quite legal."

Bewildered, she stared at him. "What?"

His smile glittered with cool intent, yet she suddenly thought she glimpsed something else hidden within it. A sadness. Or a poignancy—but then his head dipped to hers, and his kiss wiped all conscious thought from her mind.

It was a long, slow kiss, filled with the promise of what lay ahead, and it melted her with its heat. A sound came from Whitney's throat, an involuntary whisper of surrender she could no more silence than she could the race of her heart as Alex's hand closed lightly over her breast.

It was as if he had been waiting for just that moment. He drew back and looked at her through eyes as dark as the night.

"What I had in mind," he said softly, "was marriage."

CHAPTER SEVEN

WHITNEY stood before the mirror in her bedroom and stared unflinchingly at her reflection, trying to see herself as she would appear to the guests waiting in the garden below.

What she saw was a young woman with a pale face and eyes that glittered as if with fever, her mouth twisted in a tense smile. She looked either apprehensive or excited, and she knew which the assembled guests would choose.

"It's so thrilling," the wife of one of J.T.'s managers had gushed yesterday when she'd stopped by to offer her congratulations. Three days ago, Alex had made his incredible proposal.

Now, on this warm, ginger-scented afternoon, she would become his wife.

It still seemed impossible to believe. Yet, it was really happening. Here she was, dressed in the handmade gown of Victorian lace that Turner brides had worn for the past hundred and fifty years, with a little group of guests milling about below and the soft strains of Mozart drifting through the windows, no more than thirty minutes away from becoming Mrs. Alexander Baron.

"You look lovely, my dear," her father had said when he'd come to her room a little while ago. And then, for the first time since Alex had announced their plans, J.T. had looked directly into her eyes. "Are you sure you want to do this, Whitney?"

No, she'd thought. No, I'm not sure of anything, least of all this.

But it was too late for recriminations, too late for anything but facing what lay ahead.

"Yes," she'd said in a low, steady voice. "I'm quite sure."

Her father had let out his breath. "Well, that's all right, then," he'd said, and he'd left the room with almost indecent haste, muttering that he had to check the fire pit that had been dug for the *luau* that would follow the ceremony.

Whitney understood. J.T. hadn't said so, but she knew he thought that this marriage was the final inducement for Alex to grant Turner Enterprises the loan it so desperately needed.

She had let him think it. It was humiliating, but less so than the truth.

Sighing, she turned away from the mirror, walked slowly across the room, then stepped out on the *lanai*. The day was warm, with a soft breeze blowing inland from the sea. A haze of smoke from the fire pit rose faintly in the distance, smudging the blue sky.

Baskets of hibiscus and bird of paradise lined the lava-stone walkway that led through the garden, adding even more color to the already vivid splash made by the manicured sprawl of orchids, roses, and bougainvillaea. White and pink ribbons drifted in the massive branches of the koa tree that stood at the garden's heart.

It was there that she would become Alex's wife.

Suddenly, he strolled into view, part of a small group of chatting guests.

Lord, but he was beautiful to look at. Tall, broadshouldered, he had a male arrogance to him that made her pulse quicken.

Whitney put her hand to her mouth. No. She couldn't do it. She couldn't go through with it. There was still time to call things off, to...

Alex lifted his head, still smiling politely at something one of the women had just said. His gaze swept across the garden, across the lawn, to the house and then to her. Even at this distance, she could see the change that came over his features, the way his mouth suddenly hardened, the muscle that clenched in his jaw—and the unmistakable message that darkened his eyes.

Come to me, he was saying. Come to me so that we can finish whatever dark dance it is that's waited for us all these years.

She stumbled back inside the bedroom. What had she agreed to? What had she let him talk her into, that day on the road to Kona?

At first, she'd thought she'd misunderstood him.

"What I had in mind," he'd said, "was marriage."

The words had seemed to repeat themselves, over and over like a stuck record, until finally they'd lost all meaning.

Whitney had looked at him. "What did you say?" she'd asked slowly.

Alex's face was expressionless. "I said, you're going to marry me."

Her heart began to beat faster. Easy, she thought, easy. It's just some kind of bizarre joke.

"I don't think this is very funny, Alex." She spoke calmly.

"It isn't meant to be." A tight smile pulled at the corner of his mouth. "Proposals rarely are."

She stared at him. After a few seconds, she ran her tongue along her lips.

"But—but you can't be serious?"

The smile came again and then was gone just as quickly.

"Can't I?"

Tears rose in her eyes and she turned away before he could see them.

"I don't understand why you're doing this," she said. "Are you determined to find new ways to—to humiliate me?"

He reached toward her, caught her chin in his hand, and slowly urged her to face him.

"Is the thought of marrying me that hideous?"

"What kind of game is this?" she asked. "What am I supposed to do now? Am I supposed to say yes? Is that what you think? I'll say yes, and then you'll laugh and——"

"Whitney."

She twisted free of his hand. "Or is this a modern-day version of an old melodrama? I'd do a lot for my father, Alex. But I won't marry you just so he can get the loan he needs."

He laughed softly. "No. I didn't think you would."

"Good." She drew a shaky breath. "Because I'm not the trembling heroine in a badly written script."

He looked at her, his expression giving no clue as to his thoughts.

"But you *are* trembling," he said. "Why is that, I wonder?"

Color rose in her cheeks, and she swung her head away. "I want to go home."

"Don't you want to know why I've asked you to marry me?"

"No. I told you, whatever your game is, I——"

"Well, you're going to hear it anyway." He clasped her shoulders, his grip harsh. "And you're going to look at me while you do."

There was no point in arguing, not when his fingers were biting into her flesh. She turned toward him, her head high.

"I'm listening." Her voice was stilted. "But I don't think anything you say will interest me."

Alex let go of her and settled back in the seat. "It's really rather simple," he said. His voice was calm, very much in control, and she knew this must be how he sounded when he was in the comfort of his boardroom. "A man in my position—a rather successful bachelor— tends to meet a lot of women."

She smiled coldly. "Such humility, Alex. Truly, it becomes you."

"All kinds of women," he said, ignoring her remark. "But the unmarried ones—even some of the married ones—have one thing in common." His teeth flashed in a humorless smile. "They want to become Mrs. Alexander Baron."

"What a pity they don't know you better. They'd change their minds so quickly it would make your head spin."

He laughed. "You see? That's one of the reasons you'll make me a perfect wife. We've no illusions about each other, Whitney. You're not like all the creatures who fawn all over me because of who I am, pretending the only thing they've ever wanted out of life is to be my wife."

"No," she said quickly, although a little pain knifed through her heart, "no, I'll never be one of those."

Alex nodded. "So, there's the first asset. No pretense. No lying words, no promises of moonlight and roses forever." He looked at her, his mouth narrowing. "Right?"

"The first asset, you said. Is there a second?"

He nodded. "There's a second, a third, even a fourth. Would you like to hear them?"

"Certainly," she said calmly. "I'm fascinated."

"You're not empty-headed. I've always dreaded the thought of coming home at night to a woman whose interests are designer gowns, gallery openings, and not much else.'' His mouth twisted. ''You talk about business and events almost as if you were a man.''

''I take it that's a compliment,'' she said, her voice tinged with sarcasm.

''When we started out,'' Alex said, ignoring her, ''you knew next to nothing about Turner Enterprises. Now, you're damned near as knowledgeable as I am.''

''If you're waiting for me to say thank you——''

''Have I mentioned that it's time for me to have a wife? I need a proper hostess. And you've been well trained, Whitney.'' His smile was quick and sharp. ''How can I ever forget how at home you were that first night, in a setting of fine china and sterling?''

''I can give you a list of San Francisco caterers who could do the job as well,'' she said coldly. But she didn't feel cold; a strange sensation was building within her, an anticipation...

''So,'' he said pleasantly, ''what do we have so far? One,'' he said, ticking it off on his fingers. ''We've no need to play time-consuming romantic games. Two, you have an intelligent grasp of my work. Three, it's time I married. Four——''

''Stop it!'' Whitney's face trembled. ''Stop it, Alex. This has gone far enough. I'm not a—a new car that you're buying. I'm not a—a building, or a block of stock...''

''No.'' His voice was low; something in it made her fall silent. ''No, you're not.'' A shadow smile tilted across his mouth. ''And that brings me to item four.''

She knew, in the instant before he moved, what would happen next. The anger that had suffused her only seconds before fled, leaving in its place that same curling anticipation.

''Don't,'' she said, but it was too late. Alex's arms went around her and he drew her to him. ''Don't,'' she whispered, but his mouth had already dropped to hers, and in the time it took her heart to send a pulsing wave of heat through her body she was lost.

The kiss seemed to go on forever. When finally he drew back, his eyes glittered darkly.

"Despise me all you like," he said softly. "But it won't change what happens when I take you in my arms."

She drew a shaky breath. There was no point in trying to deny what happened when he touched her.

"No. But—but you can't build a marriage on—on..."

"Sex?" Alex laughed softly. "Believe me, marriages have been built on far less."

"No," she said quickly. "No, I couldn't."

His hands framed her face and tilted it up to his, and he kissed her again with a slow thoroughness that left her breathless.

"I want a home, and someone in it who knows how to make me feel welcome," he said softly. "And children to share it with. Don't you want those things, too?"

"No. I mean, yes. Of course. But—but people don't marry just for..."

Alex's brows rose. "No? Why, then?"

Whitney stared at him. The answer seemed to catch in her throat.

"For—for love."

He laughed. "What are the latest statistics? Is it one out of every two marriages that ends in divorce? Hell, among the people I know, it's closer to five out of seven. How could that happen, if all those people married for love?"

"Alex, this is insane. We can't..."

"Love is a concept dreamed up by poets and fools." His mouth grew grim. "And I am neither."

A swift pain knifed into her heart. "What do you believe in, then?"

"Facts. And a realistic appraisal of them tells me a marriage between us would have every chance of succeeding."

"No." She shook her head. "No, it's impossible."

"It would only be impossible if one of us cared for the other, because then the life we'd build together would be a lie." He paused. "And that's not the case here, is it?"

She felt the sudden sting of unshed tears in her eyes. "No," she whispered.

Alex let out his breath. "Well, then."

"I—I don't see how it could work. I just..."

"Don't you?" He drew her to him and tilted her face to his. "Let me show you," he whispered.

His mouth took hers in a long, lingering kiss, then brushed lightly against her temple and her closed eyelids.

"We'll be good together," he said softly, his breath fanning her throat as he touched his tongue to her flesh. "You know we will."

He kissed her again and again, he whispered to her, soft words not of love but of desire—and all at once she felt as if her heart were breaking.

She loved him. Oh, God, she loved him! And she always had, even in the darkest days of the past.

The realization had been stunning. She loved Alex— and now here he was, offering what she had so many times dreamed of that long-ago summer.

And yet—and yet it wasn't the same. She had dreamed of love, but that wasn't what he was offering. He spoke instead of sexual need, of shared interests—but could you build a life on that?

"Whitney?" His hands had urged her face to his. Slowly, she'd opened her eyes and met his unflinching gaze. "Will you agree? Will you marry me?"

No, she'd thought. No, of course I won't.

"Yes," she'd whispered, "yes, Alex. I will."

The reasons were wrong, but what did it matter?

The pulsing strains of *Lohengrin* rising from the garden brought her back to the present. No, she thought, she couldn't go through with it. Alex had said their marriage would work because it was built on truth.

But it would be built on a lie. She loved him, although he didn't know it and he could never know it.

"Whitney?" She looked up as the door swung open. Her father smiled and held out his hand. "It's time, my dear. Our guests are eager to see the beautiful bride."

She drew a steadying breath. "Father...."

J.T.'s smile flickered a little. "And Baron is growing impatient."

Alex, she thought, Alex was waiting.

Slowly, as if in a dream, Whitney put her hand into her father's and let him lead her from her room and down the stairs.

The ceremony was mercifully brief. The minister's voice droned, and she must have made the proper answers at the appropriate moments, because suddenly Alex was turning her toward him and taking her in his arms.

She looked at him with wide, startled eyes. "My wife," he whispered, and he kissed her.

It was only the gentlest of kisses, barely a brush of his mouth against hers. But it was different from any kiss he had given her before, and Whitney didn't want it to end.

She swayed toward him, trembling—and then, suddenly, there was a swell of music and a smattering of applause, and the unwelcome pressure of her father's hand on her shoulder.

"Whitney, my dear. Our guests all want to greet you."

The next hour passed in a blur. The wedding had been a small one—even if there'd been time to plan it, Whitney would not have agreed to the huge, formal affair J.T. had wanted. But there were still many people there—business acquaintances of her father's, of course, and people who had worked for him over the years, and even, to her surprise, some men from Alex's staff who had flown to the Big Island with their wives.

He seemed to take special pleasure in introducing her to them. "This is my wife," he said, his arm curved around her waist.

The men greeted her deferentially, the woman pleasantly enough, although she was sure she could see envy in their eyes.

Why wouldn't they be envious? she thought as she cast a glance at Alex from under her lashes. There were other good-looking men here today, but none as handsome, none with his presence. He was everything she had ever dreamed a man should be, and he was hers. He was her husband. And soon—soon...

She felt a fluttering sensation in the pit of her belly. Alex bent toward her, his arm tightening around her.

"Are you all right?"

"Yes," she said. "I just—I was just thinking that—that..."

Their glances met, and a tell-tale flush rose in her cheeks. Alex's eyes darkened until they were the color of smoke.

"Let's leave now," he said softly.

Her heart stumbled. "Yes."

"A dance. The bride and groom have to dance together," a voice called.

"Yes," another voice said, and suddenly hands were pushing them toward the wooden dance floor that had been laid over part of the lawn.

Whitney shook her head. She felt unaccountably shy. But the band had struck up something soft and dreamy, and Alex smiled and held out his arms.

"It seems we have no choice," he said quietly. "Shall we?"

She moved into his embrace slowly, her eyes downcast, and he gathered her to him closely, closely, and all at once she knew that she had waited a lifetime for Alex to hold her like this.

He whispered her name, and she sighed and lay her head against his shoulder. She felt the light press of his mouth against her hair.

"Do you realize we've never danced together before?" he murmured.

It seemed impossible that they hadn't. She fitted in his arms as if by design, and their bodies moved together with an ease and grace that suggested years of intimacy.

Years of intimacy...

Her breath caught, and somehow it was as if Alex had read her mind. His arms tightened around her, and it became hard to tell if it were the beat of his heart or hers she felt radiating through her.

"Whitney," he whispered.

Her eyes opened slowly. Still dancing, he had led her from the floor and into a quiet corner of the garden. She heard the hum of summer insects, smelled the heavy scent of frangipani.

Alex whispered her name again. The urgency in his voice sent her blood spiraling, and she leaned back in his arms and looked up.

Desire was etched into his features. It had made his mouth taut and clouded his eyes—and she almost thought there might be something else in the way he was watching her, something she had dared not hope for, and her heart lifted, swelled, until—until...

"Baron." J.T.'s voice was husky with too much Dom Perignon. He put his arm lightly around Whitney's shoulders. "You don't mind if I have a last private chat with my little girl, do you?"

Alex's expression chilled. "If that's what she wants."

Her father chuckled. "Of course she does. Isn't that right, my dear?"

Whitney tore her eyes from Alex's and looked at her father. His smile was patently false, and all at once she didn't want to talk to him. She didn't want to leave Alex's side. There was something different between them, something so new and special she was almost afraid to think about it.

But the pressure of J.T.'s arm increased. "Whitney?"

She sighed. "Yes," she said, "all right, Father." She gave Alex a quick smile. "I'll go to the house and change," she said. "I'll only be a few minutes."

He nodded. "I'll wait for you here."

J.T. led her through the garden and up the stairs, retracing the steps they had taken such a short time ago. But then she had been Whitney Turner, and now she was Whitney Baron. Mrs. Alex Baron.

Once in her bedroom, she gathered up the silk suit she was to travel in and went into the adjoining bathroom.

"I'll just be a minute," she called through the partly open door. "Alex chartered a helicopter for the flight to Oahu, and——"

"I cannot let you go through with this." J.T.'s voice was sharp.

Whitney looked into the bedroom. Her father's face was pale and grim.

"What are you talking about?" she asked.

He sank down on a chair. "The marriage. This situation. I cannot let you do it, Whitney. I thought I could pretend I didn't know, but..."

"Wait a minute." She fumbled at the buttons on the Victorian gown, then stepped free of it.

"The bastard forced you into it. He wouldn't agree to the loan otherwise."

Quickly, she slipped into the suit skirt and zipped it closed. "No. You're wrong." Her voice grew muffled as she pulled on a silk T-shirt. "That's not the way it was," she said as she came into the room.

J.T. rose and paced toward her. "Baron hasn't changed, not one whit. He's as crude and vulgar as he was years ago."

"Father—you don't understand. Alex didn't——"

"How dare he think he's good enough to become a Turner?"

She didn't know whether to laugh at her father's words or be offended by them.

"He didn't marry me so he could become a Turner," she said. "Anyway, you've got it backward. Alex hasn't become a Turner. I've become a Baron."

J.T. spun toward her. "But not for long," he said grimly. "Baron's loan came through this morning. Give me a month or two, and we can put all this behind us."

"What do you mean?"

"I've got a parcel of land on Ohau—there's a hotel chain hot to buy it."

"What has this to do with me?"

"I only need Baron's money to tide me over until the deal goes through. Then I can repay the bastard and tell him what I really think of him, and you can turn your back on this sham of a marriage and forget it ever happened."

She stared at her father in disbelief. How could her father think that she would marry Alex so he could get his loan?

"I was right about him from the start," he said. "The man's not our kind."

Whitney shook her head. "You're right," she said softly, "Alex isn't like us. He's a lot of things, but he's most definitely not a Turner." Her chin lifted. "And he never will be. I promise you that."

"Again, Whitney?" She spun toward the doorway, where Alex stood lounging against the jamb, arms crossed. His lips drew back from his teeth in a glacial smile. "Making promises you may come to regret?"

"Alex." Her hand went to her throat. "I—I didn't hear you."

"Obviously." He looked from her to J.T. "Your daughter shares your talent, Turner. She makes promises that she ought to know she can't keep."

J.T. flushed. "This was a private conversation, Baron. But I suppose knocking at a door before you open it is beyond you."

Alex threw back his head and laughed. "Where's all that cloying goodwill you've been shoving down my throat, Turner? Or do you figure you don't need it, now that you have my check in your hands?"

"Alex." Whitney stepped forward, determined not to let this day be spoiled. "Isn't it time we left?"

He looked at her. "Yes," he said finally, "it is, indeed." He smiled and she walked to his side. But, as she took his outstretched hand, his eyes went cold and flat. "We wouldn't want to miss a minute of our honeymoon, would we?"

CHAPTER EIGHT

How much had Alex overheard? Whitney cast a quick glance at him from under her lashes as the chartered helicopter covered the distance between the Big Island and the island of Oahu. Enough to make him quietly furious, that was obvious. He sat beside her staring directly ahead, his arms folded across his chest and his back ramrod straight. He might have been one of the temple gods at Pu'uhonua O Honaunau she'd been so scared of when she was a little girl. Carved of *ohia* wood, they stood glaring out to sea, silent, immobile—and unapproachable.

That was the way to describe how Alex looked now. Unapproachable. And angry. Her father had said some terrible things. But all that fawning and pretended good humor the first night he'd come to the ranch for dinner couldn't have fooled anybody.

Whitney shifted uneasily in her seat. This was not the way a marriage was supposed to begin. Honeymoons were meant for two, a bride and a groom. But this one was starting out with her father along as an unseen guest.

She looked at Alex again. Maybe the best way to deal with this was to approach it directly. If only he didn't look so formidable.

Well, sometimes the only way to get rid of an unwanted guest was to open the door and push him out.

Whitney took a deep breath. "Alex?" She waited a moment, but he made no response. "Alex," she said again, and she put her hand lightly on his arm.

He jumped as if her hand were a hot iron.

"What is it?"

"I'm sorry. I didn't mean to startle you."

"What do you want, Whitney?"

"Well, I think we ought to talk about what happened before."

He shifted his weight until he was turned toward her. "Do you?"

"Yes. I know you're angry."

His eyes focused on her face. "Angry?" he said softly. "Yes. I suppose that's as good a word as any."

She nodded. "I don't blame you. The things my father said were—they were despicable. I'm sorry you had to hear them."

A little smile twisted across his mouth, then vanished. "I'm sure you are."

"I—I don't know how much you heard..."

"Enough."

"Yes. That's what I was afraid of." She paused, then moistened her lips with the tip of her tongue. "My father's the kind of man who tends to judge other people's behavior by his own."

His brows lifted. "Really?"

"Yes. He assumes that his principles..."

Alex's lips drew back from his teeth. "His lack of principles, you mean."

"I'm not trying to defend him, Alex. I'm just trying to make you understand why he'd jump to such awful conclusions."

Alex smiled. "He was lying, then. Is that what you're saying?"

Her heart lurched unsteadily. Why would he even ask such a question?

"Lying?"

"Yes. When he said you'd married me as an inducement for the loan. You're telling me that was a lie."

She stared at him. "Yes," she said slowly. "Of course it was."

He looked at her for a long moment, and then he nodded.

"Of course it was," he repeated. "After all, why would you have agreed to this marriage if it weren't for my innate charm?"

I agreed because I love you. That was what she wanted to say. But he didn't want to hear that, although some day, perhaps, if he looked at her as he had after the ceremony, she might take her courage in her hands and...

"Well?" He smiled. "I'm waiting to hear a list of my many virtues, Whitney. Why did you marry me?"

The words were light. But there was something in his eyes, a darkness, that frightened her.

"You know the reasons," she said softly. "You said we could make a life together. A home. Children..."

"And you in my bed." His voice was cold. "Don't leave that out."

Her breath seemed to catch. "Alex? What is it? You seem—you seem..."

"Did you ever play poker, Whitney?"

"Poker?" She smiled hesitantly. "What's that got to do with anything?"

His shoulders lifted, then fell. "Do you know how to play?"

She shook her head. "No. I've never been much for card games."

"A pity." His brows lifted. "You'd be a damned fine player."

Again, she gave him a hesitant smile. She had the uncomfortable feeling that something was happening that she didn't quite understand.

"Would I?"

"Yeah." Alex stretched lazily. "You see, poker's not so much a game of cards as it is a game of nerves. You never really know what hand your opponent holds and he never knows yours. You just have to try and outfox him.''

"I'm sorry, Alex. I still don't see what——"

"Sometimes, when you play, there's a guy who's sure he's got the hand of a lifetime." He grinned. "And that's dangerous, because sometimes there's another guy at the table who's only been waiting for a fool to *think* he's got the hand of a lifetime."

"Well, but what's the difference? The player with the best hand wins, right?"

"If you match his bet, call him on it," he said softly, "then he has to show you his cards and you have to show him yours."

She gave a puzzled laugh. "It sounds like a crazy game to me."

He looked at her for a long moment. When he spoke, his voice was soft.

"But if you raise the stakes, and he can't match your bet, you don't have to reveal anything—because you've won."

Static crackled, and then the pilot's voice boomed into the cabin.

"We've arrived folks. Diamond Head's just below us, and there's the famous beach at Waikiki. We'll be touching down in just a few minutes."

Alex unbuckled his seat belt. "Last stop," he said.

Whitney looked up as he got to his feet. "Please. Tell me what this is all about."

He leaned over and put his knuckles beneath her chin. "Smile, sweetheart. We're on our honeymoon, remember?"

"Alex..."

"And I've waited such a long, long time to have you all to myself." He bent and kissed her. When he drew back, his eyes were dark. "Years," he whispered.

The 'copter settled gently on the pad. The door swung open, and a rush of diesel-tinged air swept into the cabin.

Alex jumped to the tarmac, then looked back at her. "Well?" His tone was impatient. "What are you waiting for?"

It was, Whitney thought, a very good question. After a long moment, she unbuckled her belt, rose from her seat, and followed him out of the door.

There had been no time to plan a honeymoon, not in only three days, especially since those days had been packed with appointments and meetings. Alex had suggested they fly to Tahiti, or to Australia. But then he'd mentioned, almost casually, that a friend had offered him the use of his boat.

"I told Bill it sounded great to me, but that I didn't know how you'd feel about spending our honeymoon at sea," he'd said.

Whitney had smiled. "I know this is sacrilege, coming from someone who grew up in Hawaii. But would you believe I've never been in anything larger than a catamaran?"

Alex had chuckled. "*Island Princess* is a little bigger than that. One hundred and thirty feet from stem to stern, Bill says."

"One hundred and... What is this boat, anyway? An ocean liner?"

He'd grinned. "It's an expense account perk that normally gives clients a taste of the good life."

"One hundred and thirty feet," Whitney had murmured.

"Yup. And all ours. There's a crew of eleven."

"Eleven? Just for us?"

"Uh-huh. The chef's French, the wine list's international, there's a screening room stocked with first-run films, a Jacuzzi in the master suite..."

"What? No swimming pool?"

"Sorry." Alex had assumed a look of absolute innocence. "You'll have to make do with a hot tub on the aft deck."

"A hot tub." Her sigh had been deep and exaggerated. "I don't know if I can survive all that decadence."

Alex's smile had tilted. "The question is," he'd said softly, "can you survive an entire week alone with me?"

When their eyes met, Whitney's heart had skipped a beat. It was easy to think of half a dozen teasing responses. But she'd bypassed them all and gone for the truth.

"Yes," she'd said, and Alex had gathered her into his arms and kissed her until the room spun away.

Now, as she stood in *Island Princess*'s owner's stateroom, Whitney wondered if she'd made a wise decision.

She had envisaged the yacht as being enormous and handsome. It was, but it was also as impersonal as a hotel, with Alex and she the only guests. There was something discomfiting about rattling around in all this space, just as it was unsettling to have all the crew know she and Alex were on their honeymoon.

She felt ill at ease. And it didn't help that Alex was behaving so strangely. If only he'd talk to her, tell her what was troubling him.

There was a sound behind her and she turned quickly. Alex stood in the doorway, holding a bottle of champagne and two flutes.

"I had my choice of Dom Perignon or Cristal," he said as he bumped the door closed with his hip. "So I said to myself, what would a Turner choose at a time like this?" He smiled as he set the glasses down on a small table. "Cristal, myself answered, and that's what I brought. Tell me, m'lady, was I right?"

Whitney managed a smile. "The last time I bought champagne was when I was experimenting with a new dessert for Meals in a Minute. I think the brand I picked sold for seven ninety-eight—plus a two-dollar rebate."

"Trust me." He grimaced as he eased the cork from the bottle. It made a pop and shot across the cabin. "J.T. would approve."

"Alex..."

"Whoops." He laughed as the chilled wine bubbled over the rim of the flute. "Here. Take a swallow of this and tell me what you think."

She took the glass from him and sipped the pale golden wine. "It's lovely."

"Yeah. Only the best for my bride, that's what I say." He grinned at her as he held out his glass. "What shall we drink to?"

She hesitated, and then she looked into his eyes. "To us."

Alex nodded. "Good. To us." Their glasses clinked together. "And poker players everywhere."

Whitney's smile faded. "Alex..."

"Sorry." He laughed softly. "Private joke."

"Alex, I really think we should talk."

"Damn, but it's warm in here." He worked the knot of his tie open, then unbuttoned his top two shirt buttons. "Aren't you warm, darling?"

"Alex, please. We need to——"

"Talk. Yes, I heard you." He smiled. "Drink up, first. Come on, come on. We don't want to let this stuff go flat."

She watched as he tossed back the rest of his wine, then refilled his glass. When he looked at her, she held out her glass and he topped it off.

"Can we talk now?" she asked softly.

"Honeymoon's aren't for talking, sweetheart. Didn't anybody ever tell you that?"

"Yes. But we need to... What are you doing?"

Alex chuckled. "You're a smart girl, Whitney. What does it look as if I'm doing?"

What he was doing, she thought with a sudden flutter of panic, was undressing her. He had taken the champagne flute from her hand and placed it on the table beside his. Now, he was fumbling at the buttons of her suit jacket.

"Wait. Please."

"I have waited." There was a harsh edge to his voice. "I've waited nine years. And I'm not in the mood to wait much longer."

"Alex." Whitney drew a deep breath. "I—I don't think I'm ready yet."

He laughed softly. "Hell, you were ready nine years ago."

"That's not what I—please, let's talk first."

"We're done talking." He pushed the jacket back on her shoulders, eased it down her arms, and let it fall to the floor.

"No."

He drew back and looked at her. "No?" A smile that was not a smile at all tilted across his mouth. "Is that what you said, Whitney?"

"Dammit, Alex. I don't know what you're——"

"Ah, but you do." His breath whispered against her skin as he bent his head and touched his mouth to the skin just below her ear. An involuntary tremor went through her, and he laughed softly. "Sure, you do. It's your game, Whitney, the one you play better than any woman I've ever known."

"Don't," she whispered. But the word was breathy, uttered on a sigh as his mouth moved slowly down her throat. She made a whimpering sound as he pressed his lips to the hollow where her blood pulsed just beneath the skin.

"Don't what?" He kissed his way up her throat, to her jaw, to her mouth. "Don't kiss you?" he whispered as his teeth nipped lightly at her bottom lip. "Don't touch you?" She moaned as his hand slid up her rib cage and cupped her breast. "You know this is what you want."

There was a harshness in his words that was unsettling. But she couldn't think, not when he was doing this, not when his other arm was sliding around her. She caught her breath as his hand curved across her bottom and he urged her body to his.

He was hard and aroused, and the feel of him against her made her cry out.

"Put your arms around me," he murmured.

She wanted to deny him, to say, No, I won't do it, not until we've had time to talk.

But her head was spinning. His mouth was on her throat, her cheek, her lips; his thumb was moving lightly across her silk-covered breast—and she was lost.

It was like being sucked into the heart of a whirlpool. His kisses, the feel of him, the scent of his skin, were drawing her down into a spinning vortex from which there was no escape.

This was how it had been between them all those years ago. Alex had only to touch her, and she became a wild blaze of want and need—and love. If she could just say, I want to give you my love... But he didn't want that. Not yet. She could only do the next best thing: she could show him what she felt with her mouth and her body.

Her hands slid up his chest to his shoulders, and she whispered his name.

He groaned softly. "Yes. Touch me. Lord! Touch me."

She gasped as he slid his hands under her skirt. "Oh," she whispered, "oh, Alex."

"You're so warm," he said in an urgent whisper. "So soft. You're just right for me. For this."

She moaned as he moved against her. "Wait," she said.

She drew back and fumbled at the buttons on his shirt. Alex watched her, his eyes dark and unreadable. When the shirt was finally open, he shrugged it from his shoulders and it fell at their feet.

His chest was broad, heavily muscled, with a light furring of sandy hair.

She looked up at him. "You're beautiful," she said softly.

A muscle moved in his cheek. "Am I?"

"Yes." She bent her head and pressed her mouth to his skin. His heart raced beneath her kiss.

"Whitney." His hand cupped her face and lifted it. "Is this what you want?"

Color suffused her cheeks, but she met his eyes without flinching. "Yes."

The muscle twitched in his cheek again. "Despite everything?"

She knew what he meant. What had happened between them nine years ago had been terrible. What he'd done—the way he'd used her—could never be forgotten.

But could she hold the man responsible for the actions of the boy he had been? His hands on her made thinking difficult, made reasoning impossible. No, she would not forget. But she would forgive. She sighed and gave him a tremulous smile.

She had expected an answering smile. Instead, his mouth turned down at the corners.

"Hell, why not? It's a pleasant trade-off. Daddy gets his loan. And Whitney gets laid."

The ugly word stunned her. Her eyes widened, and her face paled. She stared at him while the seconds ticked away, and then she slammed her hand against his face with such force that his head snapped back.

Silence fell across them, broken only by the sound of water lapping against the hull of the yacht.

"How dare you speak that way to me?" Her voice trembled.

"The only one who was supposed to come out of this empty-handed was me." His lips twisted. "Or did you really think getting you into my bed would make me forget I'd been played for a sucker?"

"You're going to regret all this, Alex. Because everything you're saying is——"

"Remember what I told you about playing poker, Whitney? There's always a guy at the table waiting for a fool to think he's holding all the cards." His hand closed around her wrist. "There you were, you and J.T., reaching for the stakes—and there I was, with cards that beat yours by a mile."

Her head came up. "Is that supposed to mean something to me?"

He grinned coldly. "Let me spell it out for you, lover. When your father came to me for a loan, I told him I'd sooner see him in hell."

"I'm not surprised. When you think about what happened nine years ago——"

"But then I thought it over." His teeth flashed in a quick smile. "The idea had a certain appeal, if you know what I mean."

"Yes. You couldn't resist the chance to lord it over us. Believe me, you're not telling me anything I hadn't already figured out."

"It was more than that. Hell, I wanted to see how high you and J.T. would raise the stakes." He grinned. "And now I know. No sacrifice too great. If J.T.'s firstborn had to be offered up, so be it."

Whitney grew very still. "Is that what you think?"

"What I thought was, what the hell? The Turners may be on the skids, but the name still carries some weight."

She put her hands over her ears. "I—I don't want to hear this."

"I suppose, in a way, it's funny. I mean, it's sort of a double double cross. The Turners, *père et fille*, set out to take a sucker for all he's worth." His grasp grew tighter. "And it never occurred to them that the sucker might be doing the same thing."

"Please, Alex." Her voice trembled, and she drew a breath. "I beg you—no more."

"How could I pass up such an opportunity? J.T. at my feet, sure. But the fillip was spectacular. I've wanted to expand into the islands for a couple of years now, and what better way than with the Turner name?"

"The Turner name? You wanted that?"

Alex shrugged carelessly. "Mainlanders don't realize what a closed society this is. What do you people call the upper class? *Ali'i*? Hell, I could never compete in such rarefied strata. But with you beside me it's Open Sesame."

Whitney shook her head. "No," she whispered.

Alex reached out and ran his hand lightly along her cheek. "And then, there's the bonus of having J.T.'s precious daughter in my bed." He laughed. "Well, almost in my bed. But we're about to remedy that."

His words shriveled her heart like the touch of ice. She wanted to pound her fists against his chest, scrape her nails across his face. She wanted to weep uncontrollably, to throw herself into his arms and beg him to tell her it wasn't true.

But it was. One look into his cold, pale eyes was all the convincing anyone would need.

There was nothing left to salvage but her pride. Growing up a Turner would save her now, she thought, and she gathered together all the cool dignity that was her birthright.

"No," she said quietly, "I'm afraid we're not." She wrenched free of him and took a step back. "When you've already lost the game, what's the point in playing?"

His face darkened. "I bought you," he said in a chill whisper. "And I'm damned well going to get what I paid for."

Whitney swallowed. Her throat was dry, acrid with the taste of fear. But she knew she had to stand up to him if she wanted to get out of this nightmare.

"Then you're going to have to rape me." She spoke calmly. "Because that's the only way you'll ever get me into your bed."

Alex took a step toward her. "You'd like that, wouldn't you?" he said in a whisper. "Hell, it would prove that I'm the animal you always thought I was."

Whitney lifted her chin. "Goodbye, Alex."

She turned and started across the stateroom. He was going to let her go, she thought—and then, halfway to the door, his voice came curling after her like a whip.

"Whitney. Where the hell do you think you're going?"

She stood perfectly still. "Home."

He laughed. "You *are* home, lover. Whither I go, thou goest, remember?"

"Don't be ridiculous," she said, turning slowly to face him. "This marriage is a farce."

"People have strange attitudes about their money, Whitney. They're perfectly willing to invest it in tricky situations—so long as the man who does the investing is the soul of propriety."

"Meaning?"

His mouth narrowed. "Meaning, I'm not going to try and explain a marriage that dissolves in less than twenty-four hours to my associates and clients. You are my wife. You will remain my wife, for as long as I deem it necessary."

Her throat tightened. "No."

Alex lifted the bottle of champagne and filled his glass. "I'm not giving you a choice."

"You can't do anything to stop me."

He lifted the glass to his lips and tossed the champagne back as if it were whisky.

"Can't I?" He smiled slyly. "You know that land J.T.'s planning on selling on Oahu? Come on, don't look so blank. He's going to make a fortune, selling it to a hotel chain, enough money so he can pay off the loan I made him and get the banks off his back, remember?"

She hadn't paid much attention—she'd been too upset. But yes, J.T. had said something about a land deal.

"What about it?"

Alex began to chuckle. "That's my ace, darling." He emptied the champagne bottle into their glasses, then held one out to her. "You see, *I'm* the hotel chain."

She stared at him. "What?"

"Baron's owns the company that wants to buy that land. If Baron's says 'buy,' J.T.'s out of the woods. If Baron's says 'no, thanks...'" He shrugged. "Well, I'm afraid Daddy's got a problem."

Whitney's eyes widened. "You wouldn't."

His smile never reached his eyes. "Wouldn't I?"

She stared at him in silence, and then she strode across the room and slapped the champagne flute from his outstretched hand.

"Goddamn you to hell, Alex Baron!"

Alex looked at the shards of crystal that lay scattered across the floor, and then he laughed.

"Perhaps in time, my love. But, for now, it seems my cup runneth over."

Carefully, he put his glass down on the table, walked to the door and pulled it open.

Whitney turned away and buried her face in her hands. When she looked up again, she was alone.

CHAPTER NINE

WHITNEY was sure the well-trained crew of the *Island Princess* was accustomed to dealing with bizarre requests. Still, she wondered if any of them had ever before seen a honeymoon voyage begin and end within the space of an afternoon.

Their steward made no comment when Alex rang and told him to have their luggage carried on deck.

"And phone for a taxi, please."

The steward nodded. "Certainly, sir."

Whitney thought she saw a flash of sly amusement light his face, but it was gone so quickly that she told herself she must have imagined it—until Alex stepped past her.

"Have I missed the joke?" he asked, his mouth a grim line.

The steward's Adam's apple bobbed up and down. "Sir?"

The grim line turned into a deadly smile. "You seemed to find something amusing a moment ago. I thought you might want to share it with us."

"No, sir. I was—uh, I was just..." The man cleared his throat. "I'll just get these things on deck for you, sir, shall I?"

There was a long silence, and then Alex puffed out his breath and turned away.

"Do that."

In the taxi he sat motionless, his back stiff, his arms folded, just as he had during the helicopter ride that had brought them to the yacht. Whitney hadn't heard his

124

directions to the driver. She ached to ask where they were going, but pride kept her silent.

A hotel, she thought, one of the dozens of glitzy palaces that lined the beach at Waikiki. Alex had mentioned having a suite at one of them, although she couldn't remember which. Or the Turner offices on King Street. That was a possibility, too.

But the taxi took them to the heliport. Her surprise made her break her silence.

"Where are we going?" she asked

Alex's teeth glinted in a quick smile. "To our new home, darling. Where else would a groom take his bride?"

She stared at him, baffled. "What new home?"

"Your father asked us to tell him what we wanted as a wedding gift, remember? 'Anything you like,' he said. It was an elaborate gesture but a safe one, because he never expected me to ask for anything." The cold smile flickered across his face again. "But he was wrong."

"I don't understand."

Alex looked straight at her. "The gift I want," he said softly, almost gently, "is the Turner Ranch."

The idea was so preposterous that she almost laughed. "For God's sake, he certainly didn't mean——"

"I don't give a damn what he meant." His voice was whip-sharp. "I want the ranch. And I'll have it."

Whitney clenched her hands into fists. "You won't be happy until you have it all, will you?"

Alex's eyes went flat. "That's right, sweetheart. All of it."

The helicopter ride seemed endless. Whitney didn't speak until they'd landed at the ranch and ridden to the house. Once they'd reached it, she refused to accompany Alex inside.

"You've humiliated the Turners enough," she said with bitter anger. "If you want to strip my father of the last thing he can call his, you'll have to do it without an audience."

An hour later, J.T. emerged from the house, his florid face set in grim lines.

"That son of a bitch!" When he saw Whitney, he stopped dead. "How could you have let him do this?"

"Father, I didn't..."

J.T. grimaced, then brushed past her toward the Jeep that was approaching in a cloud of dust.

"I'll be at my condo in Honolulu. If that bastard you married wants me, he can find me there."

Alex greeted her in the entry foyer. "Home, sweet home," he said with an elaborate bow. "I'd offer to show you around, but I'm sure you know the way."

Whitney put her hands on her hips. "Just what did you tell my father?"

"Only the truth, my love, that deep in your cold little heart you'd always be a Turner, and that you'd never feel at home in any house my money could buy." He paused, and his eyes met hers. "That's right, isn't it?"

"Yes," she said with hesitation, "absolutely."

Alex nodded, then turned away. "Spoken like a true lady of the manor. Now, if you'll excuse me..."

"Alex." She drew a steadying breath. "Where is my luggage?"

He stopped. After a few seconds, he swung around to face her. When he spoke, his voice was silken.

"Where would you think it was, Whitney?"

"I—I would hope it was in my old room."

"It never occurred to me to put it anyplace else."

Her heart skipped a beat. "And—and where is yours?"

He laughed. "Yes. That's the real question, isn't it?"

"Where is it?" she demanded.

He looked at her in silence while the moments ticked away. A strange feeling grew in the pit of her stomach. Trepidation, Whitney told herself. Or anger. Or—or something else...

"I've taken over your father's quarters."

It was the last answer she'd expected. Alex, in those dark rooms, cramped by somber oak furniture that had been brought to the islands in the belly of an eighteenth-century New England merchant ship?

It was an impossible image.

"No," she said slowly, "that's—that's..."

"Absurd? Inconceivable? Unthinkable?" His mouth tightened. "Yes, I'm sure you think so. But I'm the new master here. And I'd advise you not to forget it."

A tremor went through her. It was all his. The Turner house, the Turner properties, and the Turners themselves, caught in the iron grip of his fist.

How could she have thought she loved him?

Alex gave her a mocking smile. "Don't tell me you're at a loss for words, darling. That would be too much to hope for."

She blinked back the tears that were rising in her eyes.

"You're wrong," she whispered. "You'll never be master here, no matter what you do."

"I know there's some deep meaning to that little speech. But I'm afraid I'm just not interested in searching for it."

"My father was right about you all along." Whitney's voice trembled. "You haven't changed at all."

"That's where you're wrong." His smile vanished, replaced by cold contempt, and he took a step toward her. "And it means you've lost your advantage."

She lifted her chin in defiance. "I never——"

"Nine years ago," he said softly, interrupting her, "I'd have walked over hot coals to get to your bed. Now, the only way I'd want you is if you begged me to take you."

Anger, sharp and swift, obliterated caution. Whitney tossed her head.

"Hell would have to freeze over before I——"

The words caught in her throat as he moved toward her. She fell back, frightened of what she saw suddenly in his face, but her shoulders hit the wall. Alex slapped a hand against it on either side of her, and she was trapped.

"You just don't learn, do you? I've told you and told you, don't make promises you won't be able to keep."

"That's right," she said. Her heart was pounding, but she forced herself to look straight at him. "Prove you're stronger than I am."

A muscle knotted in his cheek. "That doesn't need proving." He shifted his weight, until his body was pressed lightly against hers. "But this does," he said, and his mouth took hers.

She felt nothing. The realization came instantly, and with it came a sense of relief.

She was free of him at last.

When he drew back, she gave him a cool look. "Are you finished?"

It was a mistake. She knew it as soon as she saw the darkness sweep over his face.

"Don't," she said, but it was too late. His arms were already around her, he was gathering her close to him, moulding her body to his.

"No," he growled. "I'm not finished. Not by a mile—and neither are you."

His hand twisted in her hair, he tilted her head back, and his mouth dropped to hers.

"Stop it," she said. "Alex . . ."

Later, she consoled herself by thinking that it was the way he'd kissed her that had broken through her defenses. She was prepared for anger, for a show of his strength—even for force.

But she wasn't prepared for this, for the slow, sweet touch of his mouth, the soft play of his tongue, the gentle movement of his body against hers.

"Kiss me," he whispered against her lips. "You know you want to."

No. No, she didn't. She...

His hand slipped up her rib cage to her breast. She felt her flesh swell against his palm, felt her bones begin to melt.

"I've never forgotten the taste of you," he said. "Your mouth, your throat, the soft flesh just here..."

Oh, God! How could she feel this way in his arms? She hated him, hated everything he stood for—but her hatred seemed unconnected to how she felt when he touched her.

A little moan rose in her throat, and she lifted her face blindly to him in an act of hopeless surrender.

Alex laughed softly, triumphantly. "Yes," he whispered, and he drew her tightly against him, kissing her and kissing her until the room spun away.

An hour might have passed when he finally put her from him. She had no idea. She could only stare at him while the breath rasped in her throat, and then she wiped the back of her hand across her mouth.

"You don't know how much I hate you," she said in a broken whisper.

His eyes were dark, his face without expression. "Don't I?"

"No. If you did—if you did, you'd go out that door and never look back."

Alex nodded. "Yes. That's probably what any intelligent man would do." His gaze fell to her lips and lingered there. An eternity seemed to pass before he looked up and into her eyes. "But then, I've done dumb things before, haven't I? If hatred's all that we have, we'd better learn to make the most of it."

Then he turned his back and walked away.

*   *   *

Within days, he'd made the house his. It was hard not to admire his efficiency; Whitney knew this must be the same method he used to take over a corporation. Her father's library became his office. To it he summoned the few members of the household staff.

They could stay on—at higher pay—he said pleasantly. Or they could leave, with severance cheques and letters of recommendation. The choice was theirs. If they stayed, however, it was to be understood that their loyalty was to Alexander Baron, not to J.T. Turner.

No one quit. And, within the week, new staff had been hired to supplement the old. Pearl was happy to become housekeeper, which made room for the new cook, a woman who had been schooled at *Le Cordon Bleu* and the islands' finest restaurants.

Calls went out to gourmet food shops and purveyors of fine wines. The depleted pantry and freezers in the huge kitchen were restocked, and the wine cellar once again boasted vintage bottles from the world's best vintners.

Whitney watched all this without comment. Alex had not involved her, but why would he? This was his house now, not hers—not that it had ever been hers—and he could do with it what he wished. She was surprised when, one morning, he called her into the library and announced that he had two tasks for her to carry out.

The first was to check the silverware, china, and glassware and see what needed replacing.

"Nothing will," she said. Her eyes met Alex's; this was too good an opportunity to pass up. "Perhaps you've forgotten how many generations of Turners have lived here." She smiled politely. "If anything, the house is overburdened with tableware."

"You may find J.T.'s financial distress made for some changes. And, since I plan on entertaining fairly often, adequate supplies of crystal, china and sterling will be important." His smile was as falsely polite as hers. "We wouldn't want our guests drinking out of mismatched goblets, would we?"

To Whitney's chagrin, he was right. There were only bits and pieces of the Waterford left, the Gorham sterling had been reduced to service for six, and the best set of Lenox was gone completely.

She came to Alex with lists of what needed purchasing, but he waved them away.

He was too busy for such things, he said. She was to buy whatever she wished and charge the purchases to his accounts—and that brought him to the second task which would be hers.

Alexander Baron's wife was expected to dress properly. The single suitcase of clothing she'd brought to the islands, supplemented by the things she'd left behind nine years ago, would not do.

She was to go to whatever shops she preferred and buy what she needed—and, of course, that, too, was to be charged to him.

Whitney's response was cool. "I have my own money," she said.

Alex's eyes darkened to a dangerous shade of blue. "You are my wife. And, as long as you are, I will pay your bills."

What he really meant was that he'd bought and paid for her. That was what he'd said the day of their wedding. She was a possession, like the house and the Turner lands.

"All right," she said, and then she lifted her chin in defiance. "I suppose I should ask if you have any preferences. Color, I mean, or style. You might as well get what you——"

The look on his face stopped her in midsentence. "Buy what you like. Just make certain you look the way the wife of Alexander Baron should."

And so she bought. Designer dresses, silk blouses, designer sportswear, soft kid shoes and matching handbags—she bought with a caustic disdain for price, as if each purchase were a minor victory against the man who held her captive.

She bought, even after her cupboards were filled. But, after a while, she gave it up. What was the point in extravagant charges? Alex said nothing about cost, no matter how high her accounts ran.

His only interest was in how she looked when she came down the stairs to greet his guests. They entertained almost nightly, and if the new Mrs. Baron seemed a little withdrawn it was easy to chalk it off to the shyness of a new bride—a bride with a loving, devoted husband.

Whitney wondered what her husband's clients would say if they could observe what happened after the last good night was said. Would they be shocked to see Alex's arm fall from her waist, even more shocked to watch Mr. and Mrs. Baron mount the stairs, then go to their separate rooms?

Although there were times she caught Alex watching her, his face dark, his eyes hot, and her heart would skip a beat.

Like last night.

Alex had insisted she meet him for cocktails at the Mauna Kea. She'd assumed they'd be meeting business associates of his, and she'd dressed accordingly, in a black silk Lagerfield suit with a deep V neckline.

But they'd had their drinks alone and then, to her surprise, Alex had suggested they return to the house for dinner.

Dining alone was a rare event. They ate in silence, she at one end of the burnished table, Alex at the other. When, midway through the meal, he'd suddenly spoken her name, she'd looked up in surprise.

"Here," he'd said, tossing a black velvet case to her.

She caught it and stared at him. "What's this?"

He leaned back in his chair. "Open it and see."

Jewelry, she thought as she fumbled the case open. Something gold and expensive, something showy.

Her breath caught when she saw the sapphire necklace. She looked up, speechless, and Alex smiled.

"Do you like it?"

Whitney moistened her lips. "It's—it's beautiful. But..."

"Put it on."

"No. I can't."

His breath rasped. "What do you mean, you can't? Put it on, Whitney. I want to see how you look."

But she couldn't. She kept staring at the necklace that lay in her hands, thinking how beautiful it was—thinking that this delicate fall of gold and blue fire was not like the other things he'd given her. The clothes, the household furnishings, the gold wedding band she wore on her left hand were all within the realm of reason.

But this—this was the sort of gift a man gave a woman he loved. And Alex didn't love her. He never had.

To her horror, she felt the sharp sting of tears at the corners of her eyes. She shook her head, and her pale hair fell around her face like a shield.

Alex's chair scraped back from the table. "Don't argue with me, dammit." His voice was rough as he crossed the room to her and snatched the necklace from its case. "Lift up your hair."

Her hands shook as she did as he'd ordered, shook again when she felt the light brush of his fingers against the nape of her neck.

"There." He drew back her chair. "Now, stand up. I want to see..."

He fell silent as she rose before him. For a moment, she thought he was displeased with the way the necklace looked. But when she raised her eyes to his face her heart began to race.

He was watching her with a dark intensity, an intensity that was as heated and as real as a caress.

"Yes," he said softly, "the sapphires were the right choice. The jeweler kept saying emeralds, or diamonds." He reached out and brushed a strand of silken hair back from her cheek. "But I told him your eyes were like sapphires, that they were as blue as the sea."

The room swelled with silence. He was going to kiss her, Whitney told herself. She could feel it. And—and if he did, if he did...

What was the matter with her? Alex wanted to humble her, that was what this was all about. Or perhaps he thought he could buy her. Maybe that was why he'd given her the necklace.

She waited for the familiar feeling of anger to sweep through her. But despair rose within her instead, a despair so heavy and all-encompassing that it made her throat close.

Alex stepped closer to her. "I wanted this gift to be exactly right," he said softly. "I explained that to the jeweler. I told him that..."

"...that you wanted something extravagant and impressive." Was this brittle voice really hers? She took a deep breath, then raised her eyes to his. "Well, it's all that—and more. And even if it's not exactly my style, I'm sure everyone who sees it will know how very expensive it must have been."

Her words had had all the impact she'd hoped they would. Alex's head snapped back under their force. His eyes, so dark with desire moments before, had gone blank. When he spoke, his voice was chill.

"On second thought, emeralds or diamonds will do just as well. I'll leave the jeweler's card on the desk in the hall. Exchange the sapphires for anything you like."

He'd looked at his watch, then frowned. "I've work to do. Would you ask Pearl to serve my coffee in the library?"

The card had been where he'd said it would be. But Whitney hadn't exchanged the necklace. She told herself there was no point: whatever she took in its place would still mark her as Alex's property.

And yet, just this afternoon, she'd gone to her room, opened the velvet case, and gazed at the sapphires. Their color was deep and true. If only—if only Alex had meant what he'd said.

When he telephoned to say he was bringing home last-minute guests for dinner, she was still holding the jewels in her hand.

"The manager of my Los Angeles office flew in a couple of days ago with his wife, and I'm bringing them along for dinner this evening. Will that be a problem?"

His tone had been impersonal and polite, as if he'd telephoned for last-minute reservations at a good restaurant, and Whitney had responded with equal civility.

Now, dressed for the evening in a short black silk Dior dress with a portrait neckline, she hesitated, then slipped the sapphire necklace from its case, lifted it to her throat, and looked into the mirror.

The stones burned against the dark silk like stars in the midnight sky. She stepped back further, until she could see her entire reflection in the glass, from the top of her expensively styled hair to the tips of her Maud-Frizon-clad feet.

A lump rose in her throat. She looked exactly like what she was—Alexander Baron's expensive trophy.

Her hands trembled as she unclasped the necklace and put it back into its case. There were some things you couldn't buy in this world. It was time Alex learned that lesson.

*　　*　　*

For the next three hours, she was what Alex wanted her to be—the charming, gracious hostess.

"Ah, here she is," he said when she stepped into the living room. "Whitney, I'd like you to meet the Donaldsons."

He was smiling, holding his hand out to her. But his smile was false—she'd seen the way he'd looked at her throat, then the quick narrowing of his mouth when he'd realized she was wearing the Turner pearls instead of his necklace.

"Hello," she said pleasantly. Alex's arm slipped around her waist, where it lay as heavy as a stone. "It's a lovely evening—why don't we have drinks on the *lanai*?"

The evening went well—the Donaldsons were laid-back southern Californians, and within moments Gloria Donaldson was chatting away as if they'd all known each other for years.

But, for the first time, Whitney was left to carry more than her share of the conversation. Alex was quieter than she'd ever seen him. And he kept watching her.

He was angry about the sapphires, she thought. But he didn't look angry. He looked—he looked...

"...absolutely delicious, Whitney. You must give me the recipe."

Whitney blinked and looked to her left. Gloria Donaldson was smiling brightly.

"I'm sorry, Gloria. What recipe?"

"For the salad dressing. It was super. I know I tasted sesame seeds, but what else? Ginger, maybe?"

Whitney smiled. "I think so, yes."

"And the main course. Wonderful! Swordfish, right?"

"Actually, it was marlin. It's called *a'u*. If you like, I'll ask Cook for the recipe and send it to you."

Gloria looked at her husband and rolled her eyes. "Look at this, Barry. She's gorgeous and talented—and modest, too."

Barry Donaldson grimaced. "Now, Gloria..."

"Look, you can trust me." Gloria giggled. "I won't tell anybody—except the Junior League. We're putting together a cookbook for our annual charity bazaar and I just know they'd love to get their hands on the list of ingredients that went into the marinade for that marlin."

"I really don't know. But I'll ask the cook to——"

"You mean this wasn't your recipe?"

"Mine?" Whitney shook her head. "No. Why would you think...?"

Gloria Donaldson shifted uncomfortably in her chair. "Gee, I'm sorry. It's just that Alex told us so much about you..."

Whitney stared at the other woman. "About me?"

"Well, sure. He's so proud of that catering business of yours—how you started it from scratch, how you built it all by yourself. I just thought—I mean, I just figured..."

Whitney looked down the length of the polished table. Alex's expression was impassive; he was holding his wineglass and staring into it as if it held a secret.

"Did he?" she said softly.

Gloria smiled. "Why is it men never let their wives know that they say nice things about them? Not that I'm complaining. Barry's a real romantic." She flashed her husband a smile. "That's why he took me along on this trip. It's our anniversary."

Whitney tore her eyes from Alex. "How—how nice."

"Uh-huh. We've been married two years now. How about you?"

Her husband sighed. "Gloria, for God's sake—they're newlyweds."

"Oh. Right, right. You've been married—what—two months?"

"Just over a month. We——"

"It was just one month yesterday." Alex's voice was soft, but it carried through the room. Whitney looked up. He was watching her now, his eyes dark. A tight smile angled across his face. "You might say yesterday was our first anniversary."

Whitney's breath caught. Was that why he'd bought her the necklace? Had it been an anniversary gift?

Barry Donaldson pushed back his chair. "I hate to break this up," he said, "but if we're going to get a look at those figures, Alex..."

"Yes." Alex cleared his throat. "Right," he said, glancing at his watch. "The 'copter's picking us up in half an hour."

Whitney stared at him. "Are you—are you leaving?"

He nodded. "Donaldson and I have some numbers to check. We're flying to Oahu—I won't be back until morning." A muscle moved in his cheek. "Didn't I tell you?"

She shook her head. "No. No, you didn't."

"I thought I had." His chair squealed as he shoved back from the table. Everyone rose, and Gloria Donaldson moved to her husband's side.

"Look," she said happily. "Isn't that little statue a *tiki*? Oh, it's just like the one we saw in that shop..."

The Donaldsons crossed the room as Alex walked slowly toward Whitney.

"You didn't wear the sapphires," he said quietly, while Gloria's perky voice rose in the background.

Whitney swallowed. "No."

He nodded. "I suppose you didn't have the chance to exchange them yet."

"I—I'm not going to exchange them."

"Aren't you?"

"No. I—like the sapphires. I like them very much."
Alex's eyes grew dark. "Whitney."

"Yes?"

He moved closer to her. "I have to go to San Francisco tomorrow. I'll be gone a week." He hesitated. "Will you come with me?"

Will you come with me? Such a simple request. But it wasn't simple at all, not when he was looking at her this way.

Whitney moistened her lips. "Alex, I—I . . ."

He smiled and put his hand against her cheek.

"Please," he said.

It was the simplest word of all, but it was her undoing. Their eyes met, and Whitney felt her heart leap.

"Yes," she whispered.

CHAPTER TEN

SOMEONE—Mark Twain, perhaps—was supposed to have said that the coldest winter he'd ever known was the summer he'd spent in San Francisco.

Maybe so, Whitney thought as she sat in a taxi speeding from the airport to Alex's house. The City by the Bay could chill you with dampness, then dazzle you with sunshine, and you could almost count on greeting the mornings through wisps of drifting fog.

But nothing had ever been able to dim her pleasure in this northern California city. San Francisco had always seemed to glow with a special light—until now.

The luster was gone from the glass and steel skyscrapers at Union Square, from the trim little houses that clung to the roller-coaster hills. Even the white-capped water of the Bay seemed oily and dull.

Sighing, Whitney leaned back in her seat as the taxi stopped at a red light. There was nothing wrong with San Francisco, she knew that.

It was her.

She had no business being here with Alex. Somehow, she'd let the last few minutes of the evening with the Donaldsons blind her to the truth.

A loveless marriage—the kind they'd agreed to—was one thing. But a marriage based on revenge and hate was quite another.

That was why Alex had married her, even if she'd let herself forget it for a little while.

By the time the helicopter carrying him and his guests had swooped over the house, Whitney had known she

140

could not go with him the next day. She'd made a mistake, and she would phone and tell him so first thing in the morning.

But Alex had returned early, just as she was finishing her coffee.

She'd expected him to smile when he saw her, even to be a little flirtatious. Instead, he was solemn, almost curt, and he barely looked at her.

"I'm running late," he said. "I suppose I should have called and told you what time to be ready."

"Actually, I'm the one who should have phoned you. About the plans we made last night..."

"Our plane leaves in an hour." He looked past her into the entry hall. "Haven't you had your luggage brought down yet?"

"I'm not packed."

"Well, there's no time for packing now. You can buy what you need in San Francisco."

"Alex, I don't think..."

He frowned impatiently. "Look, I'm not going to stand here and debate this. I have a meeting this evening—I'll be gone until late. You can shop then, or wait until tomorrow."

"You don't understand," she said quickly. "It's not that. It's..."

Alex took the coffee cup from her hand and put it on the table.

"Let's go."

She laughed incredulously as he drew back her chair. "Just look at me," she said. "I'm not even dressed."

His gaze flickered over her faded jeans and pale pink silk shirt. "You look fine," he said dispassionately, and then his hand was at her elbow and he was hurrying her out of the door.

During the flight, it occurred to her that she wasn't the only one who'd changed her mind about this trip.

Apparently, Alex had had second thoughts, too. He was solicitous enough, seeing to it that the flight attendant brought her a light blanket, asking if she wanted champagne instead of white wine with lunch, but for the most part he ignored her. He spent the hours between Hawaii and San Francisco frowning over the keyboard of a Compaq laptop computer, while she pretended to read the latest copies of *Time* and *Harper's*.

Now, still wrapped in silence, they sat in opposite corners of a taxi on their way to what was obviously an impossible rendezvous.

Whitney sighed. This was crazy, and it was time somebody put an end to it. As soon as she and Alex were inside his house, she'd...

She looked up as the cab pulled to the curb on Russian Hill in front of a narrow white town house.

Alex gave her a taut smile. "This is it," he said.

She touched the tip of her tongue to her lips. "Alex— maybe we should ask the driver to——"

"I'm sorry to cut you short. But my appointment's in half an hour." He dug into his pocket, then held out a brass key. "Make yourself at home. I phoned my housekeeper earlier: she promised to stop by early and stock the fridge with the necessities."

"You mean—you're not coming in?"

He shook his head. "I'm afraid not."

"But—when will you be back?"

"Ten or eleven, I'm not certain." He pushed back his sleeve and glanced at his watch. "Whitney, I'm late."

"Yes, but—but..." She let out her breath. She couldn't make her little speech now. Well, it had waited this long; surely, it could wait another few hours.

Alex reached past her to open the door. "Why don't you taxi down to Union Square later? I'll phone Magnin's and tell them you'll be using my account."

She shook her head as she stepped onto the pavement. "Thank you, but..."

His hand closed around her wrist. "You'll be here when I get back."

Were the softly spoken words a command or a request? It didn't matter: she would wait. In some small way, she owed him that.

She nodded. His eyes searched hers, and then he let go of her and sat back.

"The Mark Hopkins Hotel," he said to the driver, and the taxi pulled out into traffic.

Whitney had often wondered what kind of life Alex led in San Francisco. She knew he had offices on California Street and a house on Russian Hill. But the house had been a blur in her mind. She hadn't been able to picture it clearly, except to assume it was austerely if handsomely furnished, and would bear the chic touches that were the trademark of a professional decorator.

But she'd been wrong. There was nothing chic or even austere about this charming, sun-drenched house. It was comfortable and well lived in, and it bore the unmistakable stamp of its owner.

At first she felt like an intruder as she walked slowly through the rooms. But after a while, she became caught up in the things around her. She felt as if she were seeing Alex, stripped of all artifice.

It was a fascinating view.

He had interests other than business. That surprised her—somehow, she thought of him as being the kind of man who devoted twenty-five hours a day to his work.

But he didn't. There was a half-open closet in the hall. She could see tennis racquets on the shelf inside it, and ski boots neatly lined up on the floor.

And he collected paintings—abstract ones, mostly, great splashes of color that dazzled the eye and lifted the spirit. Whitney peered at the signatures on the canvases. She knew some of them—anyone would have—but others meant nothing to her. Alex apparently bought paintings because they pleased him, not just for their value.

She walked slowly through the hall toward a room at the far end. This had to be his study, she thought, idly trailing her fingers across a polished walnut desk and black leather chair that stood behind it. There was a whimsical metal sculpture on the desk, a series of little silver balls suspended from thin silver strands. A smile flickered across her face as she touched the first ball and set the whole line of them in rhythmic motion. Strange, but the twin of this adult toy stood on her desk in her Los Angeles office.

She wandered from the study to the living room, where clusters of little figures stood on glass shelves. No wonder Alex had scoffed at J.T.'s primitives: this collection far surpassed his. Whitney recognized some of the figures—terracotta pre-Colombian deities, ivory and soapstone Inuit hunters and their prey. The rest she could only guess at—Etruscan or Roman, she thought, or classical Greek.

There was a stereo system, too, a complicated-looking bank of audio equipment and speakers that ranged alongside shelves filled with tapes and compact discs. She smiled when she saw that his tastes ranged from Miles Davis to the Rolling Stones, Verdi and Debussy. When they'd talked about music years ago, Alex had claimed to have musical tastes even more eclectic than her own.

At least he'd been honest about that, she thought as she slipped a CD of *The Four Seasons* from its jacket. He hadn't lied just to score points with an impressionable young girl. Somehow, that pleased her.

She slid the disc into the player and pressed a button. The soft strains of Vivaldi filled the room as she wandered into the hall again.

The kitchen was spotless and equipped with every possible convenience. Whitney peered into the refrigerator. Yes, his housekeeper had been here. She wondered, fleetingly, if the woman cooked his meals, or if he took them out. A smile curved across her mouth. If there was one room in this house that didn't bear a man's stamp, it was this kitchen.

She hesitated at the stairs, and then she drew in her breath and started up. She had seen all there was to see on the lower level; she'd just take a quick look up here, then go back to the study, find something to read, and settle into a chair in the living room until Alex came back.

There were only two bedrooms. One was obviously a guest room. The other, just as obviously, was Alex's.

She stood in the doorway for a long time before finally walking slowly inside, and then she stopped and let the silence of the room surround her.

The floor was bare, highly polished, with several Navajo rugs scattered across it. There was a Navajo throw on the bed, which was king-size. Her eyes darted away from it.

The dresser surfaces were bare. There were no paintings on the walls, not even any photographs.

It was a handsome room, but impersonal. It was not a room one would spend much time in. Her gaze returned to the bed. It was difficult to imagine a woman in it, although there certainly would have been many of them, over the years. Alex was virile and attractive, he was . . .

"Whitney?"

Her heart kicked over. She whirled around, and there he was, standing at the top of the steps, watching her.

"Alex." She laughed and put her hand to her breast. "My God, you scared the life out of me." She swallowed. "I was just—I was just looking around the house. You said to make myself com... What are you doing home? I thought your meeting would run late."

He shrugged his shoulders as he walked toward her. "I rescheduled it."

She caught her breath as he brushed past her. "Rescheduled it?" she repeated. The bedroom seemed less impersonal now, with him in it. He belonged here, she thought, watching as he slipped off his jacket and draped it over a chair.

"Yeah." He looked at her. "I couldn't seem to keep my mind on business."

There was a silence, and then she laughed nervously. "Well, who could? It was a long flight, and——"

"The flight had nothing to do with it."

She looked at him. A muscle was moving in his jaw, knotting and unknotting almost in tempo with the swift beat of her heart.

"Alex..."

"My thoughts kept coming back to this house."

Her throat closed. His eyes were dark. So dark...

"Well." She swallowed hard. "Well, no wonder. This is—this is a lovely house."

He smiled a little. "I'm glad you like it."

"How could anyone not?" She was babbling like a fool, but she couldn't help it. They'd been alone dozens of times at the ranch. But this was different. *He* was different. He seemed—he seemed...

"Whitney."

His voice was low, a little husky. The sound of it sent a tremor along her spine, and she took a quick step back.

"Can I—can I get you something?" she said. "Coffee? Or—or a drink. I noticed the trolley in the living room."

"Whitney, we have to talk."

"Vodka," she said breathlessly. "Stolichnaya Cristal. Isn't that right?"

A smile tilted across his mouth. "Now, why would you suggest that?"

"Well, it's—it's what you drink isn't it?" But even as she asked the question, she knew the answer. They'd been dining together for over a month now. She'd seen Alex drink wine, an occasional Scotch or bourbon, but he hadn't asked for Stolichnaya Cristal since that first night.

He smiled as he watched the play of expression on her face. "Yes," he said softly, "that's right. I only drank it the night you and your father had me to dinner." He laughed as he loosened his tie and then opened the top button of his shirt. "It was childish, I know, but hell, what a pleasure it was to ask for something that made J.T. back up a step."

Whitney smiled at the memory. "That's what it did, all right. I couldn't see Father's face, but I could tell from the way he answered that——"

Color tinged her cheeks, and she fell silent.

"So," he said, "the cat's finally out of the bag. I thought you were on the stairs that night."

"I wasn't. I just——" She laughed uncomfortably. "Well, can you blame me? My father had just told me you were coming to dinner, and—and..."

"And you didn't know how you'd react to seeing me again after so many years."

"Yes," she said softly.

Alex nodded. "I felt the same way. The thought of seeing you again was—hell, I don't think I can put it into words."

"I—I didn't want to see you. But..."

"But, at the same time, you did."

She swallowed. This was the wrong conversation to be having. What she was supposed to be telling him was that she'd made a mistake coming here, that she was going to fly back to Hawaii...

"Whitney."

She looked up, and her heart leaped. Alex was walking toward her, his steps slow and measured, his eyes locked to hers.

"Don't," she whispered. "Alex, please—this was—this was an error. I should never have agreed to come here."

He stopped inches from her. "I lied to you."

She looked at him. Oh, God, his eyes were dark and filled with heat. If he touched her—if he touched her...

It took all the strength she had to speak. "There's no sense in talking about the past, Alex. What's done is done."

But it wasn't the past he wanted to talk about. It was their wedding day.

"All that crap about marrying you to get even," he said. "It was a lie."

She stared at him. "Why did you say it, then?"

"Because I overheard you and J.T. talking about why you'd married me."

Whitney stiffened. "Are we going to go around about the loan again? I told you, it wasn't true. My father thought that was the reason, but..."

Alex put his fingers lightly across her mouth. "You don't have to explain. I know he was wrong."

Her brow furrowed. "You know?"

A smile flickered across his face. "Remember the day I proposed? You thought I was suggesting that marriage might help smooth the loan along." The smile became a grin. "Hell, you almost killed me. It was a pretty convincing performance."

"It wasn't a 'performance,' it was the truth."

Alex sighed. "Yeah. I know."

"Then why did you believe what you heard J.T. say?"

"Look, I'm not making apologies. I mean, I am, but not for..." He thrust his hand into his hair and raked it back from his forehead. "Hell, try and see it from my angle. I walked in on this tender father and daughter scene, and then there was past performance to go on..."

Whitney's eyes flashed. "Let's not talk about past performance."

He nodded. "You're right. What counts is that I know you didn't marry me because of the loan."

She looked at him. "Why the sudden change of heart?"

He hesitated. "Remember the land J.T. wanted to sell?"

"To a hotel chain you can control?" She nodded. "I remember."

"Well, he's sold it." Alex rocked back on his heels. "Which means he's pretty much out of the woods."

"I know. He called me—he's walking on air. So what?"

Alex smiled. "So, walking out on me would have been a safe bet ever since the deal was signed."

She stared at him. "I—I never thought..."

"Exactly." His hands closed on her shoulders. "You never thought—because the money didn't mean a damn. It wasn't the reason you'd agreed to marry me."

"Let me get this straight," she said carefully. "Are you saying you're willing to believe me because I passed some kind of—of awful little test?"

"What I'm telling you is that we were both wrong."

"Yes," she said, "we were. We never should have married in the first place."

Alex's jaw thrust forward. "Will you listen to me, dammit? I know we didn't marry for the usual reasons—but they were sound ones, none the less."

A lump rose in her throat. No, she thought suddenly, no, the reasons they'd married were terrible ones. People should marry for love. And she—she had.

Tears stung her eyes. Who was she kidding? She loved Alex. That had never changed, not even during these past horrible weeks. She loved him, and she always would.

"Whitney."

She shook her head. "This won't work," she said in a muffled whisper. "I was wrong to think it would."

His hands tightened on her. "It *will* work," he said fiercely. "We enjoy the same things. We——"

"Please!" She looked up and drew a deep breath. "Don't go through it again. It won't work because—because..."

"Because we don't love each other. Is that what you're thinking?"

It broke her heart to hear him say it, but how could she tell him he was wrong? Alex had set the ground rules when he'd proposed. If one of them cared for the other, he'd said, the life they'd build would be a lie. And she—fool that she was—had agreed. She'd thought it would work; she'd *prayed* it would. But now she could see he'd been right; the fact that she loved him was changing everything.

"Look at me, dammit!" His hands slid up her throat to frame her face. "We have more than most people have to start a marriage. Do you want proof?"

Alex's mouth dropped to hers. She whimpered and tried to pull away, but his hands held her fast. His kiss was deep and filled with wanting, and, despite all her pain, all her reservations, she felt herself responding to it.

After a long time, he drew back a little and looked into her eyes.

"How many people have that between them?" he said hoarsely. His arms went around her and he kissed her again. "They write books about what happens when you and I touch each other. It's like—like fire touching tinder."

Like fire. Yes, that was what it was. A blaze of quicksilver flame that linked them together. But it wouldn't be enough, not for her. Why hadn't she realized it sooner?

Giving Alex her passion but not her love would destroy her.

Tears rose in her eyes. "No," she said desperately, "I can't. I thought I could, but..."

Alex uttered an oath as he swung her up into his arms and strode to the bed.

"Tell me that after you're naked in my arms," he said, lowering her to the mattress and coming down beside her. "Tell me it after I've kissed your breasts and your belly, after I've tasted all the sweet, secret hollows of your flesh."

She made a little sound as his fingers flew over the buttons of her shirt.

"Just let me look at you," he whispered. "Let me..." His breath caught as her clothes slipped away and fell like a discarded chrysalis to the bed. "You're beautiful," he said. His mouth brushed hers. "So beautiful." He kissed her until she was breathless, and then he drew back. "Say you want me," he said. "Let me hear you say it, after all these years."

Her eyes met his. She could lie—she had done it before. I hate you, she'd said. I'll never come to your bed, she'd said. But those lies paled when she knew she was living the greatest lie of all, by pretending that she didn't love him.

"Tell me," he whispered.

Her hand lifted to his cheek. He caught it and pressed it to his mouth and then there was no use in pretense. She couldn't lie any more. There had been too many lies between them, too many empty years.

Her arms lifted to him, and she drew him to her.

"Yes," she sighed, "I want you. I've always wanted you, Alex."

His mouth took hers in a kiss that swept away any last trepidation. Suddenly, their need was overwhelming and urgent; their fingers moved together, freeing her from the rest of her clothes, then freeing him.

Alex's hands slipped under her bottom. "I can't wait," he said. "Dear God, I can't..."

Whitney's arms tightened around his neck and she lifted herself toward him.

"Come into me," she whispered. "Please. Please, don't wait. Don't..."

She groaned as he entered her. So long, she thought, I've waited so long—and then she was beyond thought. Alex was moving within her, slowly at first, then more quickly, pulling back, then thrusting deep, taking her with him on a journey that had been too long postponed.

Something burst free deep within her. Her head fell back, and she cried out. "Yes," Alex said fiercely, and suddenly she was flying with him, rising out of herself into a place of dazzling light and color. "Yes," he said again, and she felt the hot, swift burst of his seed deep in her womb.

Tears rose in her eyes.

"Whitney? Darling, what's the matter?"

She shook her head. "Nothing," she whispered. "I'm just—I'm just..."

He gathered her to him and rolled to his side.

"Forgive me," he whispered. "I was going to make this first time last all night."

Whitney smiled and blinked back her tears. "Forgive you? For what? That was wonderful."

Alex grinned. "You mean, those are tears of joy?" He kissed her mouth. "I don't think I've ever had a better recommendation."

Her smile faded. "I don't want to know about the others," she said.

His eyes darkened. "What others?" he whispered. "How could I ever remember anyone else, after you?"

He bent his head to her breast, and she moaned softly as his teeth closed lightly on her nipple.

"Do you like that?"

Whitney drew in her breath. "Yes. I—oh. Oh, what are you——?"

"And that?"

"Alex. Alex, you can't. It's too soon..."

She cried out as he caught her hand and brought it between them. "No, it's not," he whispered.

And he was right.

A week in San Francisco, Alex had said. But the time went too quickly. The days were a blur: walks along Fishermen's Pier, drives north to the splendor of Muir Woods, south to the quiet charm of Monterey and Carmel and the breathtaking beauty of the beach at Big Sur.

They spent their evenings at home, alone in the house on Russian Hill, dining by candlelight in front of the fireplace in the living room.

Sometimes, after dinner, Alex would say, "Would you like to see a film?"

And Whitney would say, yes, that would be nice—but then they'd look at each other and smile, and his arms would close around her, and they would let the passion that always lay just under the surface close over them.

They talked, too, as they walked and as they lay in each other's arms, long conversations about all the little things that made each of them an individual.

Alex laughed at Whitney's stories about Miss Porter's Academy.

"Who'd have dreamed you were such a devil?" he said, after she told him how she and Allie had once hid all the tenth-year math texts.

His stories about the sea made her smile, too, even though she suspected that time in his life had not been half as pleasant or adventurous as he made it sound.

But they never spoke about the summer they'd shared so long ago. It was as if, by unspoken agreement, that part of their lives was closed.

It rained their last day in San Francisco. By nighttime the rain had slowed to a soft drizzle. Whitney walked into the darkened living room and stood sipping her after-dinner coffee beside the window. Lamplight in the street outside turned the mist into a spray of brightly lighted diamonds. When Alex came up behind her and slipped his arms around her waist, she leaned back against him.

"I've always liked the rain," she said softly. "I suppose that sounds crazy..."

"Would you like to go for a walk?"

Whitney turned in his arms and smiled at him. "Could we?"

He kissed her. "You can do anything. Haven't you realized that yet?"

Not anything, she thought with a sudden terrible sorrow. If I could do anything, I'd know how to make you fall in love with me.

But she didn't say that. She simply smiled and told him a walk would be lovely.

Dressed in jeans and waterproof jackets, they strolled hand in hand the length of Russian Hill. At its foot,

Alex took hold of Whitney's shoulders and turned her to face him.

"This last week has been wonderful," he said softly.

She nodded. "Yes, it has." She paused, thinking that this time tomorrow evening, they'd be back in Hawaii. The thought was strangely disquieting. "I almost wish..."

"What?"

"Nothing. I mean, it's silly. I just wish we didn't have to go back just yet."

Alex's hands cupped her face. "Maybe we don't."

"What do you mean?"

"I talked to my people on Oahu this morning. They say things are going so well, nobody's noticed I'm gone."

Whitney laughed. "Somehow, I find that hard to believe."

He smiled. "How would you like to stay away another week?"

Her eyes fixed on his. "Do you mean it?"

He nodded. "We could drive to Tahoe. I've a cabin on the lake—it's not very fancy, but..."

She sank into his arms and laid her head against his shoulder. "I think it sounds wonderful."

CHAPTER ELEVEN

THEY reached Lake Tahoe in late afternoon. "Almost there," Alex said as they turned off on a narrow dirt road that wound toward the water.

Whitney peered out the window of his Range Rover. Almost where? she wondered. She could see no signs of habitation, only stands of aspen and lodgepole pine and an occasional glimpse of the dying sun as it splashed the lake with crimson.

Suddenly, there was a clearing ahead. A small log cabin sat in its midst, looking as if it had been part of the forest forever.

Alex pulled up to the cabin and shut off the engine. He glanced at Whitney, his expression impassive.

"Well, this is it. Just let me get our stuff unloaded and I'll give you the fifty-cents tour."

She smiled as she opened the car door and stepped outside. "How about giving me the tour first?"

He shrugged his shoulders. "Sure." Their footsteps echoed dully on the wooden steps that led to the porch. "It's liable to be a little musty," he warned as he fished in his pocket for the key. "I haven't been here in months."

Whitney smiled again. "That's okay. I just want to see if it looks the way I thought it would..."

She fell silent as the door swung open. Alex reached past her and turned on the light switch.

"Well? What do you think?"

The room was bright and cheerful, dominated by a gray fieldstone fireplace flanked by a pair of comfortably worn couches that were draped with Hudson's Bay trading blankets. Navajo rugs, similar to the ones in Alex's town-house bedroom, lay scattered across the wide-planked floor.

Alex watched as Whitney walked slowly through the cabin. She paused to gaze through a door at the far end, and he cleared his throat.

"I know it's cramped," he said cautiously. "The kitchen's the size of a closet, the bathroom's hardly worth mentioning, and the bedroom..."

"...is made for midgets." She turned toward him, smiling. "Alex, it's wonderful!"

"Do you really like it? If you don't, I can always phone the Lodge and reserve a suite."

"You said it was simple, but—well, I once had this special catering job. A good client of mine got married on the spur of the moment. Her new husband had what she described as a cabin at Malibu, and she asked if I'd do her a favor and drive out there with a weekend's worth of food."

Alex elbowed the door shut and leaned back against the wall, his feet crossed at the ankles. "Don't tell me," he said with a grin. "The 'cabin' turned out to be a beach house with circular glass walls, his and hers hot tubs on the deck, a sunken pool in the back, a tennis court..."

Whitney laughed. "Nope, there wasn't any tennis court. I guess that's what made it a cabin instead of a house. So when you said you had a 'simple cabin,' I kept hoping it wouldn't turn out to be something that looked as if it'd been left over from a film set."

He held his hands out to her. She came to him and laced her fingers through his. "You like it, then?" he said softly.

"No. I don't like it." She smiled. "I love it."

"I hoped you would." He paused. "This place means a lot to me. It's my escape from the world—and until now, I've always come here alone."

The admission filled her with pleasure. She wanted to put her arms around him, lean up to kiss his mouth, and tell him how happy it made her to know that.

But she didn't dare. The words, "I love you, Alex," were only waiting to come spilling out, and she knew better than to say them. That was the only shadow on what had otherwise been the happiest week of her life.

Instead, she tossed her head and smiled coyly. "Do you really expect me to believe that the famous Alexander Baron comes here to get away from wine, women, and song?"

Alex drew her toward him. "The famous Alexander Baron," he said, matching his tone to her teasing one, "is no dummy. What would he do, he asked himself, if he brought a friend here with him and they ended up boring each other silly?" He grinned. "I did mention, didn't I, that there's no TV, no radio, and no neighbors?"

Whitney sighed. "Such deprivation." She gave him a sexy look from under her lashes. "Whatever will we do with ourselves?"

He leaned back against the wall, taking her with him. "We'll think of something," he said softly. He kissed her lingeringly. "In fact..."

Whitney put her hands against his chest and gave him a gentle shove.

"Don't you think we should get our things out of the car first? It's going to be dark soon, and if you want me to cook us a proper dinner I'll need those groceries we bought."

Alex sighed. "Now I remember why I never brought a woman here. Show 'em a little house out in the country, and their domestic urges go crazy."

She laughed. "Bachelors are all the same. Each of you is certain there's a woman with a baited trap lurking behind every home-cooked meal."

He grinned. "And with good cause, *madame*." He laughed softly and slid his hands up her arms. "Just wait until the local ladies hear you've taken me off the market."

"Uh-huh. They'll probably hunt me down."

"Yup. By this time next week, there'll be a price on your head."

"Modest, as always. Do you think they keep tabs on San Francisco's most eligible bachelor?"

He kissed her forehead. "You don't know this bloodthirsty crowd of females."

She laughed softly. "Seriously—do you think word will get around that quickly?"

"Sure. With a little help."

"Help?"

Alex nodded. "I arranged for announcements in next Sunday's papers. Didn't I tell you?"

"No. No, you didn't."

He smiled. "You don't mind, do you?"

"No, of course not."

"Good. I wanted to be sure people knew about us as soon as possible."

She smiled. "To help beat back the ladies?"

"I'd love to say yes, but the truth is that we're coming up on the benefit season, and..."

"The benefit season?"

He nodded. "That's what I call it. A little inelegant, maybe, but accurate. From September on, there's an endless round of things—balls and cocktails parties, openings, God only knows what—and, of course, people like me seem to end up on every invitation list."

"Ah," she said lightly. "I see. You're going to use me as an excuse to avoid them all. 'Sorry,' you'll say, 'but my new wife is not a party person. We won't be able to appear at your whatever, but here's our check for the amount of blah blah...'"

Alex let go of her. "If only I could," he said, raking his fingers through his hair. "But in my kind of business you don't always make deals over a desk. Being at the right place at the right time is good PR."

Whitney's smile dimmed. "Good PR?"

"You know, public relations. I hate it, but it's necessary business. So I show my face here and there..."

She felt a sudden hollow sensation deep within her breast. "I'll bet it's even better PR to have a wife in tow."

"Sure. I told you, finance is very conservative—you know, pro-establishment." He smiled and put his finger under her chin. "Don't look so downcast. Most of it's fun."

She forced an answering smile to her lips. "Have I a choice?"

Alex twisted his face into a mock scowl. "Certainly not. It's part of the job description, Mrs. Baron. You know that."

God, oh, God, of course she knew it. He needed a wife, one who'd grown up knowing how to survive the kind of evening he was describing. He'd *told* her that—but this last week, caught up in the joy of being with him, she'd...

"...now that I think of it."

She blinked. "I—I'm sorry, Alex. What did you say?"

"I was saying that it will be nice giving dinner parties at the Russian Hill house. I've always taken my guests to restaurants." He smiled. "But now that I've the perfect hostess..."

"The perfect hostess," she said softly. "And the ideal companion at all those public events. Yes, that's me."

Alex drew her closer. "Yes," he whispered, "that's you. And then, when we're alone, I'll take you in my arms, like this..."

The hollowness in her breast became a gaping pit.

"And you'll carry me off to your bed." She gave him a smile that glittered with brilliance.

"Exactly." He nuzzled her throat. "How's that sound, Mrs. Baron?"

Her heart filled with anguish. "Like—like..."

He chuckled softly. "Like what?"

"Like every boy's dream." Her voice trembled. "A lady for the ballroom, and a whore for the bedroom."

In the sudden silence, she could hear only the rasp of Alex's breath. He clasped her shoulders, then thrust her from him, holding her at arm's length in a grip so tight she could feel the imprint of each of his fingers on her flesh.

"What the hell is that supposed to mean?" he demanded.

Whitney looked at him. His face was cold, his eyes dark.

"Sorry." She tried to smile, but it felt as if her lips were glued in place. "It was just a bad joke."

His mouth turned down. "Yes. It was." His hands fell away from her and he turned on his heel and strode toward the door.

"Alex? Alex, I'm sorry. I..."

He wrenched the door open, then clattered down the steps. How could she have said such a stupid thing? Alex hadn't lied to her, he'd told her the terms of their marriage in advance. And she'd accepted them, she'd...

"Do you want these things in the kitchen or on the trestle table?"

Whitney looked up. Alex was standing in the living room holding a box of groceries.

"Alex—it was a foolish thing to say. Really. I..."

"Which is it, Whitney? The kitchen or the table?"

Her shoulders sagged. "The—the kitchen, please."

He nodded and stalked past her. After a moment, she followed. She'd made an error, but she could undo it. Her mouth firmed as she watched him set down the carton. When he finished unloading the car, she'd ask him to build a fire in the fireplace. They'd grill some steaks, open a bottle of wine, and in just a little while, everything would be fine again.

The week they'd spent in San Francisco had been wonderful. And she would see to it that this one was every bit a special.

But it wasn't. Something had died that day, and nothing Whitney did could recapture it. Conversation, which had flowed so easily, grew stilted. Little things that they'd have laughed over days before didn't even elicit a smile. And the cabin's isolation only made the strain between them more apparent.

The one place they recaptured some of what had been between them was in bed that first night. Alex took Whitney with a passion that bordered on violence. It left her spent, trembling in his arms, her heart filled with a fierce joy.

But when they came together the next night, after a long day of uneasy silences, something was missing. Whitney felt as if a part of her were standing aside, watching herself in Alex's arms. She felt constrained and tense, and that magical moment of release she had found with him from the start eluded her.

The next morning, she awoke to find Alex up and dressed. "I've been thinking," he said. "It really isn't fair of me to leave everything on my staff's shoulders for so long. Would you mind very much if we flew home a few days early?"

Whitney's heart felt as if it were going to break, but she gave him a bright smile.

"No, not at all. To tell you the truth, I'm eager to get back. I should check on those new foals."

Alex let out his breath. "Why don't you pack while I make some calls?" She could hear the relief in his voice. "I'll see if I can get us back as soon as possible."

They made a brief stop in Los Angeles, so she could vacate her apartment and arrange for the shipment of her personal possessions to Hawaii, and the sale of Meals in a Minute to her assistant.

Sally Copeland blushed like a schoolgirl when she met Alex. "Oh, he's gorgeous!" she squealed to Whitney as soon as they were alone. "You must be so happy."

Whitney nodded. "Very."

But she wasn't happy, she was miserable. Her relationship with Alex, which had bloomed so brightly in San Francisco, was dying. And there didn't seem any way to save it.

She tried everything she could think of. During the long flight home, she chattered about an article she'd read in *Business Week*. Alex's responses were polite, but it was obvious he wasn't interested in conversation. When they touched down in Hawaii and were waiting for their helicopter charter, she asked him his plans for one of the sugar plantations they'd visited together. Again, he answered politely. But as soon as she stopped talking he opened his newspaper and buried his nose in it.

Eventually, she gave up saying anything, and they made the last leg of their trip in silence.

That night, they dined by candlelight. The cook had prepared a special homecoming meal of grilled *mahimahi*, and Alex opened a vintage bottle of Perrier-Jouet to go with the Hawaiian fish. But the meal might as well have been gruel and water for all the taste it had on Whitney's tongue.

They spoke hardly at all, except to make stilted conversation about the food. Then, over coffee, Alex cleared his throat.

"I assumed you wouldn't feel comfortable in rooms that were your father's."

Whitney looked up. "No. No, I wouldn't."

He nodded. "I'll have an architect in next week to see about making a couple of the guest rooms into a master suite."

"Fine," she said softly.

Alex glanced at his watch. "I've some work to attend to. Why don't you go on upstairs, and I'll join you as soon as I can?"

Her head came up. "But—but you just said..."

"I said we'd create new rooms for ourselves. Until then, I expect to spend the night in your room on occasion." There was a sudden, hard glint in his eyes. "Unless you had a better plan."

"No. That's fine. I..." She fell silent. Of course that was what he would do. What had she expected? Alex would come to her bedroom, just as he had so many years before.

She swallowed, then pushed back her chair. "I'm very tired," she said. "I'll—I'll probably be asleep by the time you come upstairs."

He gave her a tight smile. "I won't be very long, Whitney. I promise."

Alone in the safety of her room, she shut the door and sank back against it. Why had the thought of sharing this room with Alex stunned her? He was right about her father's quarters, she'd never have wanted to sleep there.

Her gaze flew around the room. She'd done nothing to change it in the two months she'd been home: it was almost ludicrous to think of Alex here, surrounded by pink and white ruffles. The room still looked as if it belonged to a teenage girl—the one who'd waited here, nine years before, for the sound of Alex's footsteps.

Whitney sank down on the edge of the bed. That long-ago night, Alex had come in through the *lanai*. Now, he would come boldly up the stairs. That was his right, as her husband.

That was all that had changed, though. Alex hadn't loved her then, and he didn't love her now. He wanted her, yes, and he had a use for her—but those things had been true in the past, too. Painfully true.

Her throat closed. She wasn't up to facing him tonight. Not tonight. Quickly, she stripped off her clothes and put on her nightgown. She hurried to the bathroom, washed her hands and face, brushed her teeth, and did it all so rapidly that she was breathless by the time she scrambled into bed. And it was just in time: she heard the door opening just as she pulled up the blankets.

Her heart hammered as she closed her eyes. Alex's footsteps approached the bed softly. She heard him pause.

"Whitney?"

She didn't stir. After a moment, she heard the faint hiss of cloth, and she knew he was getting undressed. When he padded to the bathroom, she rolled over on her belly and buried her face in the pillow. Why hadn't she thought to shut off the light? There was only one lamp, glowing gently beside the bed, but it would have been better if the room had been dark, if there were no danger of Alex seeing her face.

The bed creaked as he lay down beside her. He moved towards her, put his arm around her waist, then drew her back into the warmth of his naked body. For a moment, she held herself rigid. But then she felt the heat of him seeping into her flesh, and she sighed. It felt so good to have him hold her, so right to be in his arms.

He whispered her name again as he rolled her on to her back. Slowly, she opened her eyes and looked at him as he leaned over her.

"I knew you were awake," he said softly.

She moistened her lips with the tip of her tongue. "Actually, I was—I was almost asleep."

His gaze moved slowly over her face. "Did you really think you'd be able to sleep when it's our first night together in your bed?"

An icy fist clamped around her heart. It wasn't their first night in this bed, she thought, he'd been here before, he'd taken her in his arms...

Whitney turned her face away. "Alex," she whispered, "I'm sorry. But—but I'm awfully tired."

He smiled and bent toward her. "How tired?" he said, and he brushed her mouth with his.

Her heart turned over. Never too tired to love you, she thought. But what he wanted from her had nothing to do with love. It never had.

She closed her eyes. "Very. All those hours of flying always leave me feeling drained."

"What you need," he said, his breath feathering her cheek, "is a good night's sleep."

"Yes. That's—Alex. Please..."

His lips touched her ear. "To do that, you need to be completely relaxed."

"I am relaxed. I..."

He cupped her chin in his hand and turned her face to his. "Let me relax you, darling," he whispered. He kissed her, gentle little kisses that offered much more than they asked. After a while, she sighed and her lips parted.

"That's it." His tongue moistened the curve of her mouth. "Just lie back and let me do everything."

"Alex. Alex, I really don't think..."

"That's right." His voice was husky, his hand gentle as he slid her nightgown from her shoulder. "That's right, darling. Don't think. Don't do anything except lie in my arms and let yourself drift."

His mouth was like hot silk along her throat. She made a little sound as he kissed the curve of her breast, and when he drew her nipple into his mouth she moaned.

He looked up at her. His face was taut, his eyes dark. "You see?" He smiled. "You're not too tired, are you?"

"Alex..."

He cupped her breast in his hand, then touched his tongue to the erect nipple. "Not for this," he whispered. His hand slipped up under her gown and moved lightly on her flesh. "Or for this."

A tremor went through her. "Please," she murmured, "please..."

"Please, what?" His voice was thick. "Please make love to you? Is that what you want, Whitney?"

"No. I—I—oh. Oh, yes. Yes..."

He rose above her. "Put your arms around me. And touch me. You know you want to."

Tears rose in her eyes. That was what he'd said that long-ago night. How well he knew her, and how well he used that knowledge. He'd always known how to get what he wanted from her. Once, it had been the twenty-five thousand dollars that he'd extorted from her father. Now, the prize he claimed was far bigger. He already had the Turner ranch, the Turner name, and soon—soon he'd have her on his arm, he'd have her opposite him at his table in San Francisco, and he would always have this from her, as long as he wanted it, because just his touch was enough to set her aflame.

"Whitney. Put your arms around my neck."

Blinking back her tears, she lifted her arms and wound them tightly around him, hating him and loving him at the same time for the terrible power he held over her.

"Open to me," he whispered, and she did, crying out her pleasure as he tasted her, moving beneath him as he touched her, until finally nothing mattered except this moment and the man in her arms.

Alex entered her, sheathing himself in her warmth. She cried out and rose to match his thrusts with her own. At last, on the brink of release, she arched her hips and cried out his name.

I love you, Alex, she thought.

"I want you so much," he whispered—and his words shattered against her like crystal against stone. She fell back, back from the edge of sweet oblivion, back to a reality that she could not escape, and she lay immobile beneath him, trapped within the earthbound confines of her body.

Alex shuddered, then fell against her, his body slick with sweat. She lay unmoving while his breathing slowed, while his heart ceased its mad gallop, and then she shifted her weight.

"Am I hurting you?" he whispered. He rolled over, taking her with him, and cradling her in his arms. "What is it?"

She shook her head, afraid that if she tried to speak, she would burst into tears instead.

"Whitney. Please, talk to me."

She closed her eyes and turned her head away from his dark scrutiny.

"The light's too bright. Would you mind turning it off?"

He hesitated, and then he reached toward the bedside table and turned the switch. The room plunged into darkness.

"Now, tell me. What's wrong?"

"Nothing. I just—I guess I'm more exhausted than I thought."

Alex's breath was warm against her face. "You're as tense as a coiled spring," he said, brushing tendrils of silken hair back from her face.

"I'll be all right. I just need a night's sleep."

"Not yet. Not while you're like this."

"Alex . . ."

He kissed her lightly on the mouth, then on the throat, then on each breast. His hand moved across her midriff.

"Just let go," he whispered. His thumb grazed the damp curls low on her belly, his fingers brushed lightly between her thighs. "That's it. Let me help you, darling. I want this always to be good for you."

Because this was his power over her. The thought was ugly, but no more so than the truth, that sex without love was all she would ever find in his arms.

And it wasn't enough. Dear Lord, it would never be enough, and she had been a fool to have thought it would.

"No!" Her voice was sharp; she put her hands against his chest and twisted away from him. "No, I don't want anything, Alex, except that you leave me alone." Her voice broke. "Is that too much to ask for?"

Silence rose around them, broken only by the rasp of Alex's breath.

"No." His voice was chill. "No," he repeated as he shoved the covers aside and got out of the bed, "it's not too much to ask at all."

A little flicker of alarm raced along her skin. She sat up against the pillows.

"Alex? What are you doing?"

It was a useless question. She could see what he was doing; the moon had risen, and there was just enough light so she could see that he was pulling on his pants and gathering up the rest of his clothing.

"Go to sleep, Whitney. I've disturbed your sleep enough tonight."

"Alex . . ."

He stalked across the room, pulled open the door, then slammed it behind him. After a long, long time, Whitney lay down again and buried her face in her pillow. Sleep finally stopped her tears.

When she came down the next morning, Alex was gone. He'd left word with the housekeeper: he had an early appointment and a full day. She was not to wait dinner for him, he was sure he'd be late.

And he was, that day and the next, and virtually all the following days. Their lives fell into a routine that only differed from the one they'd established during the early weeks of their marriage in that Alex brought no guests home to dinner.

Whitney had no idea how he entertained his guests, just as she had no idea if he attended the events on the northern California "benefit circuit" he'd joked about. He made trips to San Francisco—lots of them—but he never again asked her to accompany him.

She knew what was happening. Alex had never set foot in her bedroom after that first night. As far as he was concerned, the flame that had linked them had died. He wanted a woman in his bed, not a statue. She couldn't blame him for that, nor for the anger he held so tightly in check.

She had violated the terms of their agreement, and she knew it was only a matter of time until he demanded a divorce. And she would give it to him, even though the thought of losing him was as agonizing as a blow.

She loved him too much to cling to this sham of a marriage.

Now, on this rainy autumn night, she sat propped against the pillows in her bed, sipping a cup of weak tea. She'd come down with some kind of bug, maybe because she was living under so much stress. She ached all over, but that wasn't as bad as the persistent nausea.

It didn't help that she kept thinking about what would happen when Alex arrived home tomorrow. She stirred uneasily, remembering his phone call earlier.

"We've things to discuss, Whitney," he'd said, "and I don't want to put them off any longer."

She sighed as she put her teacup on the bedside table. A divorce, that was what he wanted to discuss. But she couldn't survive a talk, not without breaking down, and that was the last thing she wanted to do.

She'd make things easy for him. "Alex," she'd say, "we've nothing to talk about. I'll see a lawyer immediately, and..."

She jumped as the bedroom door swung open. Her hand went to her throat: Alex was standing in the doorway, watching her.

"You scared the life out of me," she said.

"I seem to make a habit of doing that." He stepped into the room and shut the door after him. "Remember that first day we were in San Francisco? You were in my bedroom and I came flying up the stairs." He grinned rakishly. "I could hardly wait to get to my beloved wife's side."

Whitney stared at him. "Alex? Are you all right?"

"Fit as a fiddle. Aren't you going to ask me what I'm doing home tonight?"

"Are you sure you're all right? You look..."

Drunk! That was how he looked. His eyes were glazed, and there were patches of unnatural color high on his cheeks. She felt a flutter of fear in her belly.

"Why don't you go wash up while I put my robe on, and then we'll go downstairs and I'll make you some——"

"Coffee." He chuckled as he walked toward her. "That's what you were going to say, wasn't it?"

She shoved the covers back and reached to the foot of the bed for her robe. "Coffee sounds fine," she said, although it didn't, just the thought made her want to throw up. "Give me a minute, and..."

His hand clamped around her wrist. "No."

Whitney swallowed. Alex's smile was gone, leaving his mouth grim and narrow. "Let go of me, please."

He cocked his head to the side. "Always the lady," he said softly. "'Let go of me, please,' she says—even though her heart's racing like that of a hunted doe."

His hand tightened on her as he drew her up from the bed. A faint scent of whisky wafted toward her.

"You're drunk."

"His mouth twisted. "No. Not drunk, lover. Just gently anaesth—anaesthi..."

Whitney's chin lifted. "Drunk," she said coolly.

Alex chuckled. "Lubricated—for what lies ahead."

Her heart stumbled. "Nothing lies ahead. Just get out of my bedroom."

"Your bedroom." His lip curled. "Right. Forgive me, I forgot that this bedroom belongs to the lady of the manor."

"Alex..."

She caught her breath as he tugged her towards him. "Well, it's my bedroom, too, sweetheart. I pay the bills now, not Daddy."

Whitney gritted her teeth as she tried to twist free. "Get out of here, Alex. We'll talk tomorrow, after you're——"

An oath as hard as the hand that held her exploded from his lips.

"I don't want to talk," he said, and his mouth clamped down on hers.

Fear raced through her. His body was hard, his arms imprisoning. The whisky taste of him sent a shudder through her.

Alex drew back and caught hold of her shoulders. "Kiss me, damn you. Kiss me as if you meant it."

Bile rose in her throat. "Please," she whispered, "don't do this. I—I don't feel well."

His face grew dark. "I disgust you, is that it?"

"No. I just—Alex, please."

His hands cupped her face, and he bent to her. His mouth ground against hers; she felt the sharp bite of his teeth, then tasted the salt tang of blood. A wave of nausea radiated out from the middle of her belly.

"I beg you," she whispered.

"That's right, beg me. I want to hear you beg me to take you. Because I don't want you any more, damn you! Do you hear me, Whitney? I don't want you!"

Tears rose in her eyes. There it was, the thing she'd dreaded, the thing she'd known had been coming. Alex wanted her out of his life. God, oh, God...

"Well?" He thrust his face toward hers. "I'm waiting, lover. What have you got to say now?"

A despair greater than any she'd ever imagined swept over her, but somehow she managed to look at him and say the words that had to be said.

"I'll contact a lawyer first thing in the morning."

Alex's breath hissed between his teeth. "Fine. Just tell him I want this over with fast."

"Yes." She nodded. "I will. And I'll have my things packed and ready to be shipped as soon as I get settled somewhere."

His face twisted. "Don't bother," he said. "The house is yours. Hell, it always was. This pompous pile of bricks is Turner property—I never belonged here."

He stared at her for a long moment, and then he turned and strode toward the door. Whitney put her hands to her mouth. Alex, she thought, Alex, don't leave me. I love you.

"Alex." His name whispered from her. She took a step forward, her arms outstretched, and he turned. "Alex," she said again, and then nausea ballooned within her. Her eyes rolled up into her head, and she collapsed in a heap at his feet.

CHAPTER TWELVE

WHITNEY stared at the doctor in disbelief. "No," she said softly, "it's not possible."

The doctor shrugged. "My dear Mrs. Baron, nothing is impossible, no matter what precautions one takes."

"You could be wrong, though. Surely there are other tests...?"

"Even the greenest practitioner can determine a healthy, normal pregnancy. Seven months from now, you and your husband will be proud parents."

"My husband—does he know? Have you told him?"

The doctor nodded. "Of course. I spoke with him last night, after I'd examined you." He looked at her as he snapped his medical bag closed. "Remember now, bed rest for the next few days, and then you can begin to resume normal activities."

Normal activities. Was divorce a normal activity for a woman who'd just learned she was pregnant?

The doctor frowned. "Have you a question, Mrs. Baron?"

Yes, she thought, oh, yes. She had many—but none that he could find answers for in the bottom of that little black bag.

"No," she said, "no questions."

"Well, then, I'll be on my way. Your husband's outside, pacing the hall like a caged tiger." He smiled. "He's eager to see you, and I don't blame him. He's very concerned."

Whitney shut her eyes as the door swung closed. She could just imagine Alex's concern. He'd just begun to divest himself of a wife he didn't want, and now it turned out she was carrying his child.

His child. Her hand went to her belly. Alex's baby was growing within her. Those wild, sweet nights in his arms had produced a life.

Tears stung her eyes. The terrible poignancy of it twisted, knife-sharp, in her breast. There would be a legacy from that week in San Francisco, after all. A baby she hadn't planned on, a baby no one wanted...

No. No, that wasn't true. She wanted this baby. It was hers, hers and Alex's. It was all that remained of what might have been.

The door flew open, and there he was, looking as if he hadn't slept all night. There were dark crescents under his eyes, his shirt was rumpled—but it was the look on his face that told her just how upset he was. She had expected anger, but this was something different. He looked—he looked like a snake, coiled and ready to strike.

"Well," he said, "this sure as hell makes a mess of things, doesn't it?"

"No," she said quietly, "it doesn't. Nothing's changed."

Alex put his hands on his hips. "Would you mind explaining that?"

"The doctor wants me to stay in bed for a few days. But as soon as I'm on my feet, I'll find a place..."

"A place?" His voice was soft as a cat's. "What kind of 'place'?"

"What do you mean, what kind? A place to live."

"You're going to have this child, then."

"Yes."

He gave her a cool smile. "Let me get this straight. You're going to leave me, find an apartment, and have this baby."

"That's right," she said calmly, although she didn't feel calm. Beneath the sheets, her hands knotted together, the fingers twisting with anxiety.

"And how will you support yourself while all this is happening?"

"I won't ask you for anything, if that's what you're——"

"Answer the question," he said sharply. "You'll need money for rent, for food, for medical care. How will you manage?"

Whitney shrugged. "I—I'll get a job. Believe me, you won't be responsible for my support."

"A job doing what?"

She looked at him. "This is not an inquisition. I told you, I'll manage."

His jaw jutted forward. "You mean, Daddy will manage. You'll trot off to J.T. and he'll take care of you and my child."

She sighed wearily. "Alex, please. I'm tired."

"Is that the plan? Your father will raise my son?"

For a second, the words made her heart lift. My child, he'd said, my son. But then she looked into his eyes and she knew they were only words with no special meaning beyond what her unhappy heart tried to give them.

"Answer me, Whitney."

"I have answered you. This baby is none of your concern."

Alex was beside the bed in a few quick steps. His hands clasped her shoulders, and he half lifted her toward him.

"You're wrong," he said through his teeth. "What's in your belly belongs to me. *I* will make the decisions for it, no one else. Do you understand?"

She knew he was trying to intimidate her. Everything about him was meant to frighten, from the cold steel of his voice to the pressure of his fingers on her flesh. But it wouldn't work—not this time.

"You can't stop me from having my baby," she said quietly.

His breath hissed. "Is that what you think I want to do?"

She swallowed. "I thought—I thought..."

He looked at her while the seconds ticked away, and then he let go of her.

"I'm a lot of things," he said softly. "But I'm not quite the son of a bitch you'd like to think I am."

Whitney ran her tongue along her lips. "You want me to have the baby, then?"

His lips drew back from his teeth. "I hate to disappoint you, my dear wife, but the answer's yes. I want this child. And I've no intention of turning him—or her—over to you and J.T."

Her pulse stumbled. "No court will give you custody," she said quickly. "I don't care how much money you have."

He drew back, straightened to his full height, then put his hands on his hips. "Well, well. Even Whitney Turner admits money can't buy everything." He laughed softly. "Don't worry, lover. I don't intend to give you the luxury of a custody fight."

"Then what are you talking about?"

Alex smiled. "Prepare yourself for another disappointment, darling. There's not going to be any divorce."

She stared at him in amazement. "No divorce?"

"That's right, no divorce. No child of mine is going to be raised the way I was. A kid needs a mother and a father—and a home that I've provided, not this—this mausoleum." Dazed, she watched as he turned on his heel and strode to the door. At the last second, he stopped and swung towards her. "By this time next week, we'll be living in a house that doesn't know the meaning of the Turner name."

Whitney stared at him while she tried to sort out all the things he'd said.

"Wait a minute. Alex—wait!" She sat forward in the bed. "You can't just make all these decisions and—and..."

He laughed. "Can't I?"

The door shut after him. Drained, she fell back against the pillows and closed her eyes.

He was absolutely right. He was Alexander Baron, and he could do whatever he damn well wanted.

He was wrong about being out of the Turner house in a week. It took almost a month before he found the house he wanted, a sprawling contemporary tucked away in the hills above Honolulu. Despite its proximity to the city, the house was isolated, only accessible by helicopter or by a narrow, rock-strewn dirt road that snaked up from the flats via a breathtaking series of loops and hairpin turns. It would have to be repaired and resurfaced, Alex said, after the rainy months ended.

Under other circumstances, Whitney knew she'd have loved the place. The house was spacious and airy, and it was beautifully furnished—Alex had managed to convince the finest shops on the island to deliver whatever he needed virtually overnight. There were several outbuildings: a garage that housed a Blazer, and, when Alex was home, a Range Rover, a stable that was home to a pair of Arabians, and a gardening shed. An oval swimming pool gleamed like a blue jewel behind the house; around it lay a garden alive with tropical flowers of incredible color and variety.

The estate was fully staffed. Alex had hired a housekeeper, a cook, a maid, a gardener, a stable boy and a chauffeur. Whitney, he said, was not to prepare meals, make a bed, weed the garden, saddle a horse, or even drive herself anywhere.

"What am I supposed to do, then?" she'd demanded.

He'd given her a swift, impersonal smile. "Watch over my child." It was useless to tell him that this child was doing just fine without her help. The doctor had given her a clean bill of health, but Alex seemed convinced she was fragile. Not that he was concerned about her—it didn't take a genius to figure out that it was the baby's welfare that drove him.

Sometimes, she felt a twinge of jealousy for this unborn infant she carried within her. How could Alex feel such love for it and none for her? But the feeling never lasted long. She loved this baby, too—it had been conceived, if not in love, then in joy. There was some solace in that.

Alex was rarely home. The "benefit circuit" was in full swing in San Francisco: she supposed he was busy making his appearances. He had a new secretary, too, one she'd never seen. But she'd heard the woman's soft voice and husky laugh once when she'd answered the phone, and an icy fist had clamped around her heart. Had Alex so quickly found someone who would fill his arms, now that she didn't?

No divorce, he'd said. But he hadn't promised fidelity, and she had no reason to expect it. Their marriage was over. They were a pair of strangers, sharing the same last name. And, if she was still helplessly in love with her husband, what did that have to do with anything?

It was, Whitney knew, a hopeless way to live. And it would be a terrible life to offer a child. Children needed more than a parent, or even two parents. They needed love—who knew that better than she? She tried telling that to Alex, but he was unyielding. He didn't love her, he didn't want her—but he would never let her go.

It was like living trapped inside a maze, Whitney thought on this sunny late autumn morning as she wandered slowly through the garden. There had to be a way out, but where was it?

She shook herself briskly. She had to keep busy; if she didn't, she'd go crazy. Riding was out—Alex thought it too strenuous, and he'd given orders she was not to take out either Arabian. And if she tried working in the flowerbeds, the gardener, also following orders, would politely but firmly put a stop to it.

She sighed. A trip into town, then. There was a shop that sold hand-embroidered baby clothes, she'd gone there last week, and...

But that was out, too. The Blazer needed work. The chauffeur had had a nasty scare yesterday when the brakes had almost failed. He'd made an appointment to have the car serviced at the end of the week; until then, she had no transport.

Whitney sighed. Well, she'd go for a swim. Swimming was good exercise. Not even Alex could fault that.

She went into the house and to her room. Quickly, she stripped off her light cotton dress and her underthings. As she passed the mirror, she caught a glimpse of herself, and she paused, then turned and stared.

Her body was really changing now. Her breasts were full, her belly rounded, and there was a softness to her face and eyes that was different. She smiled, then put her hands on her stomach. The baby would begin to move soon, the doctor had said. She could hardly wait to feel him kick.

Her smile faded. Alex would never feel his child move in her womb. To do that, he'd have to touch her. And she knew he would never willingly do that again. He could barely bring himself to look at her. She'd seen the change that came over his face when he thought she wasn't looking, as if—as if he'd seen something he hadn't wanted to see.

"Whitney? I'm sorry to bother you, but..." She gasped and swung toward the bedroom door just as Alex entered the room. He stopped in midsentence; his eyes swept over her before he gritted his teeth and turned away. "Dammit, what are you doing walking around like that?"

Tears filled her eyes. "No one asked you to come walking in," she said. Her hands shook as she pulled on a pair of pants and a cotton T-shirt. "Didn't anyone ever teach you how to knock?"

His shoulders lifted as he drew a deep breath. "You're right. I apologize."

"All right," she said after a moment, "I'm dressed. You can turn around now."

By the time he did, she was seated at her dressing table, combing her hair. He watched her for a moment, and then he cleared his throat.

"I came back from the mainland a day early."

"Yes. So it would seem." Her voice was curt, and she could only pray it hid the sorrow she felt. God, the look on his face when he'd seen her! How ugly he found her, how repulsive.

"I'm going to have to fly to New York for a few days."

She yanked the comb through her hair. "Well? Why tell me?"

He sighed. "Look, I didn't come here to pick a quarrel. I simply wanted to tell you that I'd be gone for a while. A week, perhaps. If you have to reach me..."

"I know. Call your office and tell your secretary."

"My secretary will be going with me."

Whitney closed her eyes. "I—I see."

"You can reach me at the Waldorf Towers."

She nodded. "All right."

"Just call and ask for me. Or for Miss Palmer..."

She spun toward him. "I said, all right, Alex. I know where you'll be, I know your secretary will be with you."

Her voice trembled and broke, and she held her breath until she was sure she could speak again. "Is there anything else?"

Alex stared at her, and then his mouth twisted. "No," he snapped. "No, dammit, there's nothing else. Goodbye, Whitney."

She waited until the door shut after him, and then she buried her face in her hands. Things couldn't go on like this, she had to tell him that once and for all. Alex was concerned with her physical health, but he didn't give a damn for her mental state. She was going to come apart at the seams soon—and she couldn't. She had her child to think of.

She blew her nose, then got to her feet. "Alex," she called. Barefoot, she hurried down the stairs. "Alex, when you get back from New York..." The entry foyer was empty. She pulled the door open and rushed into the driveway.

The Range Rover was still in the driveway. Then he hadn't left yet. But where was he?

The gardener was weeding the rosebushes that flanked the driveway. "Ito, have you seen Mr. Baron?"

The man looked up and nodded. "Yes, missus. He just left."

Whitney frowned. "What do you mean, he left? His car's still here."

"Mr. Baron say to tell John to take a look at it. He say it have a flat."

A flat. Yes, there it was, a dead tire. But if Alex had left the Range Rover...

A chill hand seemed to close around her throat. "Ito? Did my husband—did he take the Blazer?"

The old man smiled. "Yes, missus. He take your car."

The Blazer. The Blazer, with brakes that had already failed. Alex would reach the first hairpin curve, he'd put his foot on the brake pedal and, instead of slowing, the car would pick up speed, it would lift off the road in a slow, dizzying arc, then tumble to the rocks below...

"Oh, my God!"

Whitney raced down the driveway, around the house and to the stable. The sound of her breathing seemed as loud as the sound of the blood thrumming in her ears.

"Please," she whispered, "Oh, please, please, don't let anything happen to Alex."

The Arabian gelding nickered softly as she slipped on a halter and bit, then led him from the stable.

"Come on," she said, "come on, Abdullah, come on, boy." It was years since she'd ridden bareback, but she grasped the long, flowing mane and scrambled onto the horse's back without hesitating, and then she kicked her heels into his flanks. The startled animal took a few hesitant steps forward and Whitney, clutching the reins, leaned low over his neck and kicked him again.

The horse thundered out of the stable and onto the road. Whitney heard the gardener call after her, heard the stable boy's frightened cry, and then all she could hear was the wind.

Later, when she tried to reconstruct what happened, she could recall only bits and pieces. She remembered the road unwinding ahead, the sun glinting on Alex's car, the first hairpin curve waiting in the distance, like the coiled length of a sleeping snake. She remembered looking off to the fenced meadow that paralleled the road until just before that terrible curve, remembered urging the horse into the soft grass for a desperate race against the clock.

She bent low and put her mouth to the Arabian's ear. "Come on," she whispered. "You've got to do it, boy."

She remembered sailing over the fence, the squeal of brakes, the horse's frantic whinny—and then, blessedly, there was only darkness.

*　*　*

She was dreaming, and in the dream, Alex was holding her close. He was talking to her, too, he was asking her to open her eyes and look at him. Please, love, he said, please.

She sighed and snuggled deeper into the warmth of his arms. The voice—Alex's voice—kept urging her to awaken. But she didn't want to. If she did, this wonderful dream would end. She would open her eyes and find herself alone, the way she always did. Alex would be gone.

"Whitney. Look at me. Come on, love. Open your eyes."

Sighing, she did what he'd told her to do. She was in a room—her room. In her bed. But this was no dream. Alex was really here. And he was holding her.

Suddenly, it all came rushing back. The car, the road, the horse...

She began to struggle frantically. "Hush," Alex said, holding her close to him. "You're all right."

"My baby?"

"The baby's fine, too."

Whitney lay her head against his chest. "I—I was afraid I wouldn't make it in time," she whispered.

She felt the sudden tensing of his body. "And you damn near didn't," he said. His hands clasped her shoulders, and he held her at arm's length. "What the hell kind of stunt was that? Haven't I told you and told you not to ride?"

Tears stung her eyes, and she blinked them back. "I wasn't riding. I was trying to stop you. The car—the brakes..."

"Do you realize what might have happened?"

She swallowed convulsively. "I—I never thought, Alex. There wasn't time."

"No. You never think. That's the trouble with you, Whitney. You do whatever the hell you want, and——"

A sob burst from her throat. "Don't scold me," she begged in a broken whisper. "Please, don't. I know you're angry because I endangered the baby, and I swear, I didn't mean to. But—but I had to stop you. I had to..."

"You could have died, do you know that?" His hands tightened on her. "But if you had—if you had..." He groaned, and suddenly his voice was hoarse with anguish. "If you had," he said, "I'd have died, too."

Time seemed to stand still. She could hear the steady beat of his heart beneath her ear, hear the sound of a bird trilling in the garden outside, and then Alex tilted her chin up. His eyes were dark, and soft with a light she had only dreamed of seeing in them.

"Why did you risk your life for me?"

"Because—because..."

"Tell me, my love."

My love. He had called her his love. Dared she tell him? No. She couldn't—but what more was there to lose? Her pride, yes, but what was pride in the face of hope?

It had been easier to leap onto the back of the Arabian and gallop off with the wind, but finally Whitney gathered her courage and said the words she had longed to say for so many years.

"Because I love you," she said softly.

Alex lifted her face to his and kissed her, over and over again, until her mouth was soft and warm beneath his.

"If you knew how many years I've waited to hear you say those words," he whispered. "You were my first love—and you've been my only love ever since."

Her heart swelled with a joy so intense it was almost too much to bear. But part of her held back. She wanted to believe him. But—but...

"If you'd loved me nine years ago," she said uncertainly, "you wouldn't have—you wouldn't have hurt me so."

He sighed as he stroked the hair back from her temples. "I guess I expected too much of you—but I didn't know you were only sixteen. If I had, I wouldn't have asked you to defy your father and run away with me."

Whitney drew back and stared at him. "What are you talking about? You never asked me to do that."

"Of course I did. I asked the housekeeper to give you a message. I told her it was urgent."

Whitney shook her head. "I never saw Emma. She was gone when I came down the next morning. My father said she was unreliable."

Alex closed his eyes, then opened them. "I waited and waited, down near the stables the next night. But you never came."

"Oh, Alex. I'd have come to you, if I'd known you wanted me. I'd have gone to the ends of the earth ..." She stopped short. "But—but you couldn't have been waiting for me, not after you'd taken the money from my father."

His brows furrowed. "What money?"

"The twenty-five thousand dollars. The money you demanded as your price for not seeing me again."

"What?"

The shock contained in that single, explosive word echoed through the room. Whitney looked into her husband's eyes, and suddenly she knew that there was more to what had happened that long-ago night than either of them had ever imagined.

"Alex." She put her hands on either side of his face and looked into his eyes. "My father told me you'd set out to seduce me, that you'd set things up so he'd walk in on us that night."

"Jesus. And you believed him?"

"You believed I chose not to run away with you."

There was a silence, and then Alex caught her wrists in his hands.

"Listen to me," he said fiercely. "I loved you. It was why I couldn't bring myself to make love to you in the stables—hell, I knew you deserved better than a bed of hay. I wanted everything to be perfect."

"Oh, Alex . . ."

"I told your father that I was going to ask you to be my wife. And he—he laughed, Whitney. He said you'd just been playing games, that you'd no more marry a nobody than the man in the moon. He said you had an unfortunate tendency to play around with the hired help——"

"It's not true. You should have known he was lying."

"I didn't believe him—not then. But the next night, when I waited and waited . . ."

Whitney lifted her face and pressed a kiss to his mouth. "Oh, my love," she whispered. "We've wasted so many years."

Alex's arms closed tightly around her. "When I found out Turner Enterprises was in trouble, I told myself the chance for revenge was too sweet to pass up. But I was kidding myself. I'd just been waiting for the excuse to come to you again—I knew it as soon as I saw you."

"The day you proposed was like a dream," she said softly. "And then, that week in San Francisco, I was so happy—but then, when we got to the cabin at Tahoe, I began to think about—about all the reasons you'd married me, and I knew I loved you too much to go on pretending. That was why I said those awful things, why I couldn't make love to you any more."

Alex sighed. "I thought you hated me. I told myself I had to let you go—and then we found out you were pregnant. God forgive me, but it was all the excuse I needed to stop you from ever leaving me."

Whitney turned her face up to him and they kissed. When they broke apart, she put her hand against his cheek.

"Alex? Is—is your secretary very pretty?"

Alex grinned. "Why, Mrs. Baron, I do believe you're jealous."

"Just tell me. Is she?"

"Yup. And her grandchildren think so, too."

Whitney's brows rose. "Her grandchildren?" A smile tilted across her mouth. "Really," she said, and she laughed. "Grandchildren, huh?"

Alex smiled. "She says grandchildren are a wonderful discovery." He touched his finger to Whitney's mouth. "If she's right, maybe having a little Turner/Baron incorporation will soften J.T. around the edges."

Whitney sighed and looped her arms around her husband's neck. "Well," she said dreamily, "there's only one problem left to solve."

He grinned. "Yeah?"

"You've got to stop treating me as if I'm made out of glass. The doctor says we pregnant ladies are pretty tough customers."

He nodded. "I know I overdid it. But I'd come so close to losing you so many damned times..."

Whitney smiled. "You're never going to lose me, my love. I swear it."

Alex drew her toward him. "Well, then," he said softly, "we're just going to have to figure out a way for you to convince me that you're not going to break."

Her hands moved to the back of his head, and she brought his mouth down to hers. They kissed for a long, long time; when they finally drew apart, Whitney's eyes were shining,

"I think I know just how to do that," she said.

And she was right. She did.

The BARBARY WHARF six-book saga continues with Book
Five, A SWEET ADDICTION. Guy Faulkner and Sophie Watson
have both been abandoned by the people they love, but is that
reason enough to find themselves in each other's arms? It isn't
for Sophie. And it isn't the kind of solace Gina Tyrrell wants
from Nick Caspian, either—despite the fact that she's becoming
increasingly confused about her feelings for the tall, handsome
man. But love them or leave them, these men just won't go away!

A SWEET ADDICTION (Harlequin Presents #1530)
available in February.